First published in Great Britain in 2021 by Cassell,
an imprint of
Octopus Publishing Group Ltd,
Carmelite House,
50 Victoria Embankment,
London EC4Y 0DZ
www.octopusbooks.co.uk
www.octopusbooksusa.com

An Hachette UK Company
www.hachette.co.uk

First published in France © Gallimard, collection Hoëbeke, Paris 2020

Copyright © Octopus Publishing Group Ltd 2021
Translated from French by Simon Jones

Distributed in the US by
Hachette Book Group
1290 Avenue of the Americas
4th and 5th Floors
New York, NY 10104

Distributed in Canada by
Canadian Manda Group
664 Annette St
Toronto, Ontario, Canada M6S 2C8

ISBN 978-1-78840-337-5

A CIP catalogue record for this book is available from the
British Library.

Printed and bound in china

10 9 8 7 6 5 4 3 2 1

For English edition
Editorial Director: Joe Cottington
Creative Director: Jonathan Christie
Assistant Editor: Sarah Kyle
Translator: Simon Jones

CODEX METALLUM

Illustrations
Førtifem and Mathias Leonard

C CASSELL
ILLUSTRATED

CONTENTS

CONTENTS

INCANTAMENTA DIABOLI

THE DEVIL'S
INCANTATIONS

 **HALLUCINATIONS**

Have you ever closed your eyes and pressed your fingers into your eyeballs? Blueish spots come to life and swirl endlessly in the darkness. Although nature and our bodies are capable of producing such phenomena, it is the taking of hallucinogenic drugs that allows our brains to fully explore these matrices, which are as fascinating as they are disturbing. Music and drugs have often gone down the same paths – and this can be seen in the genres that would, much later, give birth to heavy metal. The experience offered by the psychedelic rock of the 1960s and 1970s was primarily an internal and spiritual one. The use of drugs, despite the risks it involves, can allow us to see things that do not exist and to subvert reality to the point of bringing us face to face with a fascinating distortion of it. The idea of visiting other worlds by passing through the doors of perception is one of the most significant aesthetic elements of psychedelic rock – and such perceptions are transposed and projected on to numerous artworks of the period. Texas band **The 13th Floor Elevators** were led by the wild **Roky Erickson**. Their first album, released in 1966, bears the evocative title *The Psychedelic Sounds of the 13th Floor Elevators*, and is a visual and musical archetype of this craze for hallucinogenic substances. As well as leading to two encounters with the authorities, the excessive use of drugs caused Roky to be admitted to a psychiatric hospital, where he received electroconvulsive therapy. **Cream**, **Jimi Hendrix**, **Hawkwind** and more… numerous musicians and bands, well into the 1970s, used drug-induced hallucinations to create music and associated visuals. The imaginary world surrounding drug taking was often linked to a certain hedonism, a way of escaping the depressing greyness of reality, and this is one of the reasons why the visuals are generally grotesque, highly coloured and original. There is an almost childlike aesthetic in the naive (in the artistic sense of the term) imagery that appears on these album sleeves. Molecules such

as LSD and DMT change the perception of colours, and give the impression of having access to new realms of vision. Although the end of the hippie era would curb this tendency, today, in a slightly similar approach, stoner metal groups use highly charged, coloured visuals in homage to the aesthetic of psychedelia. Indeed, 'stoner' is itself a slang word denoting a regular drug user.

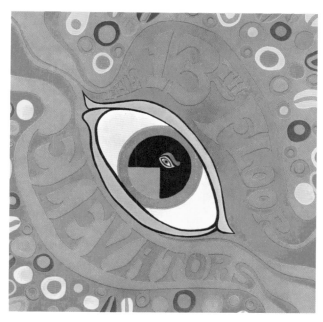 

The 13th Floor Elevators – *The Psychedelic Sounds of the 13th Floor Elevators*
Cream – *Disraeli Gears*
Acid King – *Middle of Nowhere, Center of Everywhere*
The Jimi Hendrix Experience – *Axis: Bold as Love*

PURPLE

The albums *Master of Reality* by **Black Sabbath** and *Burn* by **Deep Purple** were released in 1971 and 1974 respectively. Reflecting their nebulous content, their sleeves have two features in common. The typefaces are undulating, aiming to emulate the curves of a thick cloud of smoke or the outline of a ghost floating through the night. But there is also, importantly, a desire to bring to the fore an electrifying deep violet colour. Doom metal, with its slow tempos, deep chords and profound themes, is the type of music that could accompany a trance or a ritual, connecting us with a form of arcane musical mysticism. And that same violet colour is found in numerous doom metal artworks, to the point that some have made it a recurring theme, such as the Italian **Paul Chain**, a living legend of the underground who brought prestige to slow, bewitching metal music during the 1980s. And prestige it was – for, historically, the colour purple has been associated with the idea of rank and wealth. It was an imperial colour and difficult to make – it was created using pigments found in certain molluscs. In ancient Rome, wearing purple was the prerogative of the nobility, and there was a time when only Julius Caesar was allowed to wear it. Violet also appears on ecclesiastical robes and altar cloths. Francis Bacon's famous painting *Innocent X* depicts the pope wearing a robe of this colour. It was said that purple had the virtue of pacifying the dead and soothing the devils in Hell. In a different context, purple is connected with organic matter, for certain organs have a colour that comes close to it, as does coagulating blood. In the spectrum of colours, violet is obtained by mixing red and blue, two quite distinct hues. On the one hand there is the red of roses, blood and passion; on the other, the blue of reason, and that sense of the infinite we experience at the sight of the sea and the sky – expanses of which we cannot see the end. Purple is, therefore, a colour that,

in a way, forms a link between our bodies and the divine, between the flesh and the heavens. It is also the final colour of the rainbow, the last hue before the unknown, which **Sortilège** convey very well in *La Huitième Couleur de l'arc-en-ciel* (The Eighth Colour of the Rainbow). Violet, too, is the colour associated with Jupiter, the largest planet in our solar system. All this symbolism fits perfectly with the telluric heaviness of this music and with the mystical – almost magical – charge it sometimes claims to carry.

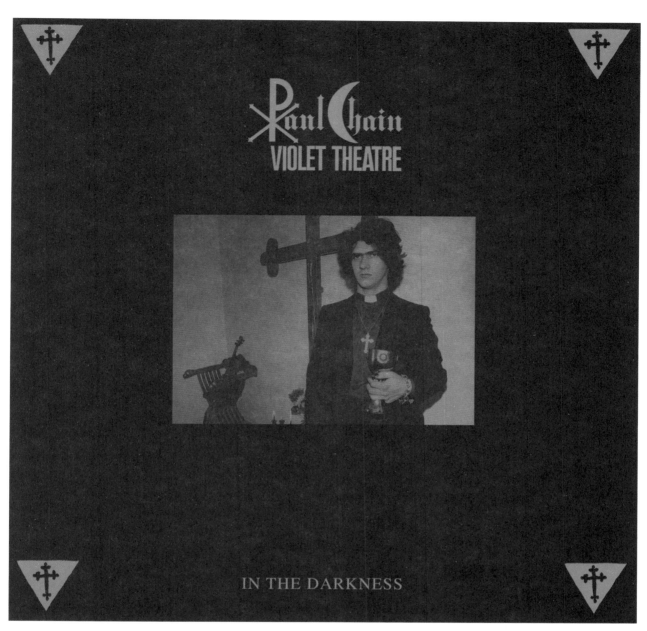

Paul Chain Violet Theatre – *In the Darkness*
Electric Wizard – *We Live*
Black Sabbath – *Master of Reality*

The starting point of metal is generally held to be **Black Sabbath**'s eponymous album, released on 13 February 1970 in Britain and 1 June that year in the United States. At the centre of the record sleeve image is the strange figure of a woman, standing like a witch in the middle of her wood – evoking the spirit of doom metal even before that subgenre was more precisely defined, years later. The photo arouses curiosity, and seems like a dark omen. Very soon afterwards, **Black Widow** referenced witches too. The concept was to be explored by many bands playing rock, metal, black metal and, above all, doom metal, a subcategory in which women – via the figure of the witch – were more commonly represented than they were elsewhere. By virtue of their place in folklore and their position as enemies of the Inquisition, witches immediately fitted in with the symbolism of this music. Since they were the victims of mass murder, on the orders of mad clergy who saw in them the expression of a pagan freedom that absolutely had

to be suppressed, some artists viewed them as libertarian, mystical heroines whom it was fitting to glorify through dark, spellbinding music. Other groups preferred to highlight, on their record sleeves and in their album titles, the darkness that emanates from the *Malleus maleficarum*, a genuine treatise written by two inquisitors on the punishments and methods of torture to be inflicted on the so-called witches. This dark and violent aspect of religion is an area that some artists seek to explore, for metal as a musical genre took shape partly in opposition to religion and the morality of conservative elites. In later years, as certain groups have found themselves the subject of finger-pointing by fundamentalist moral authorities, we can draw a sort of parallel with the experience of the witches (though without being burned at the stake). Indeed, in the United States, the merciless hounding of communists during the Cold War was dubbed a 'witch-hunt'. The witch is a powerfully enduring symbol in our collective unconscious, and movements such as Wicca lay claim to this even today. In a wider sense, music contains a form of magic equation. It causes us to feel so many mysterious things that drawing an analogy between musician and magician comes naturally.

Black Widow – *Black Widow*
Black Widow – *Sacrifice*
Acid Witch – *Witchtanic Hellucinations*
Black Sabbath – *Black Sabbath*
1782 – *She Was a Witch*
Witch Charmer – *The Great Depression*

The cross is the supreme symbol of Christianity. It is the instrument of torture by which Jesus Christ was put to death. It symbolizes the sacrifice Jesus made, and above all his forgiveness of humanity. The cross is, therefore, supposed to remind us of the goodness, wisdom and greatness of the Son of God. Before it became associated with metal music, the inverted cross was known as the Cross of Saint Peter. When he himself was being crucified, Saint Peter asked that the cross be turned upside down as a sign of respect for Jesus, for he did not regard himself as worthy of being put to death in the same way. It was much later that the inverted cross came to be used as an anti-Christian motif. Turning a symbol upside down means that its values are being rejected, or even that the opposite of the doctrine it's associated with is being advocated. The inverted cross also strongly resembles a sword – synonymous with killing, not with eternal forgiveness. In rock music it dates back to 1969, with **Coven** and their *Witchcraft Destroys Minds & Reaps Souls*, a rock album in the same vein as others being produced in the 1960s, but with a theme – that of a witches' coven – that was unprecedented at the time. The album's visual elements are full of anticlerical references, from the famous 'horns up' hand sign (devil's horns formed with the index and little fingers) to the sacrifice of the Virgin Mary and, naturally, the inverted cross. **Tony Iommi** of **Black Sabbath** wore the inverted cross around his neck, and it also appears in the gatefold of the band's first album, which popularized this symbol among lovers of rock and, subsequently, hard rock. Later on, **Venom**, the first generation of black metal (**Hellhammer**, **Celtic Frost**, **Sarcófago**), the second generation (**Mayhem**, **Gorgoroth**, **Taake**), some doom groups, such as **Witchfinder General**, and some death metal groups all made use of the Christian cross in their logos, album sleeves and promotional photographs.

Going for full-scale provocation, **Marduk**, on the sleeve of their *Fuck Me Jesus*, made completely different use of the crucifix, calling to mind a similar scene in William Friedkin's movie *The Exorcist*. By extension, in horror films and movies dealing with demonic possession, an inverted cross indicates the presence of the Evil One, who cannot bear to see a crucifix the right way up. He inverts it to express his blasphemy and to desecrate it, stripping it of its divine power.

Sarcófago – *I.N.R.I*

Coven – The back of *Witchcraft Destroys Minds & Reaps Souls*

SIGILS

Like occultism, metal is for the initiated and is not always directly accessible. In order to access its secrets, one must first master its imagery, themes and culture. It is not uncommon for bands to highlight certain esoteric symbols. Some of these are almost a part of pop culture, such as the famous number of the Beast: the prize for this goes to **Aphrodite's Child**, a group including **Vangelis** and **Demis Roussos**, who released an album with the title *666* that featured unambiguous graphics. Other records call attention to different symbols, such as the sigil of Lucifer, to which **Imprecation** dedicated an EP. The aim here is to use obscure symbols that speak only to the initiated, those who have devoted themselves to a quest for knowledge and understanding. A sigil carries within it a whole imaginary world: that of secret societies and long-lost knowledge, of runic culture, and of signs that conceal an ancestral black magic. With just a symbol, it is possible to invoke the imaginary world of sacred geometry, as **Dissection** do with *Reinkaos*. The symbol that is most emblematic of the genre is the inverted pentagram. While a pentagram the right way up represents a form of divine elevation, its inverted counterpart embodies the rejection of that spirituality. Moreover, the branches of this pentagram form the shape of a goat's head. This symbol is all the more significant in metal music because it appeared on the sleeve of the historic *Welcome to Hell* by **Venom**. Since metal groups were assumed to have satanic intentions and be seeking to pervert the young, what could be more exciting than to take advantage of that assumption and use it to frighten right-thinking people? Some bands overloaded their album sleeves with symbols or even intermingled them. This can be seen with *The Wild Hunt* by **Watain**, which superimposes a lyre, a trident and Hebrew symbols to create a cryptic image. The symbol's

meaning is not often understood. It repels as much as it attracts. It is an enigma that demands to be deciphered. In aesthetic terms, the symbol often takes the form of a fine, stylized engraving. But it can also be more flamboyant and aggressive, as on the magnificent sleeve of *The Nocturnal Silence* by **Necrophobic**. It should be noted that the pentagram has also been used as an amulet by Gerald Gardner and his Wicca movement as a sign of recognition between members. It matters little that none of these groups is truly well-versed in witchcraft or the academic study of ancient sigils... All these signs connect with a forgotten past, a form of pagan occultism, a language that acts as a key to unlocking a disturbing, unknown world.

Dissection – *Reinkaos*
Aphrodite's Child – *666*
Imprecation – *Sigil of Lucifer*

CHAOSPHERE

The Temple of the Black Light (formerly the Misanthropic Luciferian Order) is an occult order to which some Swedish black metal groups, such as **Watain**, **Dissection** and **Arckanum**, gravitated. This order was headed by the highly discreet Frater Nemidial, who wrote a book containing supposedly satanic precepts described as 'anti-cosmic', as well as some of the lyrics in *Reinkaos*, the final album by **Dissection**. The groups that belonged to this movement employed somewhat more specialized symbols linked to this 'chaosophic' philosophy, or to closely related parallel trends: the sigil of Lucifer, the trident, the Leviathan Cross and the anti-cosmic pentagram. This whole sometimes gruesome façade masked ideas that were eminently serious, for they could be linked to the suicides of Jon Nödtveidt (**Dissection**) and Selim Lemouchi (**The Devil's Blood**, **Powervice**, **The Temple of Azoth**), as well as to certain crimes committed during the 1990s by members of the Swedish scene. According to the anti-cosmic precepts, order is embodied by the universe we inhabit. Order is destiny as it unfolds in our dimension, governed by immutable physical laws. As for chaos, it is everything and nothing, the infinite possibility of conceivable scenarios. Therefore, absolute chaos is nothingness – what there was before the zero point of our universe; even before the first atom saw the light, even before the creator of the universe began to bring it into being. The sigil that seems to correspond most closely to this occult philosophy is the Chaos Cross, also known as the Chaosphere. It is in opposition to the symbol of law: a single arrow. **Dissection**, however, never made use of it. Originally, the Chaos Cross was created by writer Michael Moorcock in his novel *The Eternal Champion*, in which questions about the cosmic order and chaos frequently appear. The symbol was then taken up by some modern occultist movements. In fantasy literature, chaos is the embodiment of absolute evil. It is a demonic entity that imposes itself through violence, to change souls and matter. For **Bolt Thrower**, known for their fervent love of the board game *Warhammer 40,000*, the Chaosphere symbol echoes this supernatural dark energy. The Swedish band **Craft** makes no concessions: their third album is entitled simply *Fuck the Universe*, and the Chaos Cross, red on a black background, holds majestic pride of place. In the

cases of **Quo Vadis** and **Helstar**, the Chaosphere is enhanced with other esoteric symbols, reinforcing its mystical aura, while for **Meshuggah**, it takes on an almost surrealist shape. With its image of a cage containing a human brain, the sleeve of their album *Chaosphere* brings us back to our condition as living beings that are prisoners of a mathematical determinism. Although the Chaos Cross is not the most common sigil, it is the one that carries the greatest metaphysical and philosophical charge. It symbolizes the questioning of existence itself, and the vertigo it can cause when one is immersed in this thought.

Quo Vadis – *Infernal Chaos*
Bloody Sign – *Chaos Echoes*
Crimson Midwinter – *Random Chaos*

GOATS

What has the poor goat done to find itself saddled with a satanic aura? Nothing, other than to have been used in a parable in the Gospel according to Matthew, which says that when God returns to Earth, he will separate the faithful sheep from the goats, which have not believed in him. Ever since, the goat has been adopted as the animal that is the emblem of the devil. The source for Baphomet, the horned humanoid immortalized by the occultist Éliphas Lévi, is less clear. It supposedly has its origin in the Crusades, and the Knights Templar were even accused of worshipping it in secret during their trial. But it was with the rise of modern occultism that Baphomet gained recognition, to the point of being revisited as a blasphemous entity in the metal aesthetic. The goat has become a recurrent figure of the genre, and personifies the devil himself. Charged with mysticism and sexuality, it appears on multiple black metal record sleeves in designs by Chris Moyen, as well as on those of cult groups such as **Dark Funeral**, **Dimmu Borgir**, and **Vital Remains**, and its head is sometimes set within a pentagram. The connections between the devil and a composer's musical inspiration were not born with metal. Many talented artists have made a pact with the devil. In 1713, Giuseppe Tartini made himself into a legend by relating how the devil came to him in a dream and taught him a violin sonata – the *Devil's Trill Sonata*. It has even been said of some bluesmen, notably **Robert Johnson**, that they owed their talent to Satan, who supposedly came in person to bargain for their souls in return for giving them virtuosity on the guitar. It has also been said that **Elvis Presley** was possessed by the devil when he moved his hips. Thus Satan is part of rock and roll's DNA and, in a case of hyperbole that is characteristic of metal, Baphomet has become a veritable symbol. From the early 1980s, the horned idol appeared in the new wave of British heavy metal (**Witchfynde**, **Angel Witch**, **Venom**) as well as on stage with **Iron Maiden**, when the latter began to perform *The Number of the Beast*. **Slayer** also featured an inquisitorial humanoid goat on the cover of their cult album *Reign in Blood*. Subsequently, black metal and doom metal, the two subgenres most prone to occult tendencies, made extensive use of it. In a less stylized context, sometimes an actual goat – as in, the herbivorous mammal – has featured on an album sleeve: less iconic, but just as full of allusions.

Nunslaughter – *Goat*
Witchfynde – *Give 'em Hell*
Goatsnake – *Trampled Under Hoof*

On the sleeves of the albums *Come an' Get It* by **Whitesnake** and the appropriately named *End of Eden* by **Amberian Dawn**, the serpent is shown with the apple that he will persuade Eve to eat – the very fruit that led to the expulsion of humankind from the Garden of Eden. In Milton's *Paradise Lost*, it is Lucifer himself who assumes the disguise of a serpent to offer the apple to the two fallen lovers. Since this is one of the few incarnations of the devil in the Bible, many groups have depicted the reptile in a demonic light, as a tempter – for example, **Obscene** in *Sermon to the Snake*. It is sometimes even phallic, as on the astonishing sleeve of *The Serpent's Gold* by **Cathedral** and that of *Lovehunter* by **Whitesnake**. Furtive, deceitful, dangerous and manipulative… in the collective unconscious, the serpent hypnotizes and lures us to the dark side: it is the famous 'Trust in me' chanted by Kaa in the Disney movie *The Jungle Book*. It is an animal that is feared in all cultures, and not only because of its deadly venom. However, if the serpent is considered from a perspective other than the Christian one, it also embodies more mystical and ambivalent concepts. It is a figure that symbolizes duality. Although the reptile kills, it can also cure, for its venom has extremely powerful properties. Indeed, the caduceus, which is used as an emblem of the medical profession, features a snake. Through the shedding of its skin, the serpent experiences in its flesh the almost alchemic alternation of life cycles and rebirth, leaving behind its old, dead skin in order to be reborn anew. The snake is also the symbol of eternity and renewal, as shown by the uroboros, the famous image of a serpent biting its own tail. Highly prominent on many album covers, the uroboros may be subject to different aesthetic approaches: realistic, mythical, deathly and more… and, every time, the concept strikes us with full force. That is the power of symbols. **Manam**, **This Spring of Death**, and **Earth Messiah** have all made concept albums called *Ouroboros*. Finally, the serpent can take on divine or mythical forms. Sometimes bands seek inspiration from the Hydra of Lerna, as in the case of **Testament** and the

three-headed serpent on the cover of their album *Brotherhood of the Snake*. Here, again, is a symbol of rebirth – if one tried to cut the head off the Hydra, two heads would grow back in its place. The artwork for *Ov Lustra* by **Sun Speaker** features a magnificent plumed serpent that flies and screams over the sun. The serpent of ancient Egypt also recurs in the work of groups such as **Nile**, and on the mysterious sleeve of *Serpents of the Nile* by **Scarab**. The serpent is, without a doubt, a symbol with many interpretations, as capable of representing gods as embodying the devil. Like the Antichrist, the serpent is coiled up underground, lurking in the burrow of extreme kinds of music that are, like him, cryptic, fascinating and dangerous.

One Tail, One Head – *Worlds Open, Worlds Collide*
Pantera – *The Great Southern Trendkill*
Whitesnake – *Love Hunter*

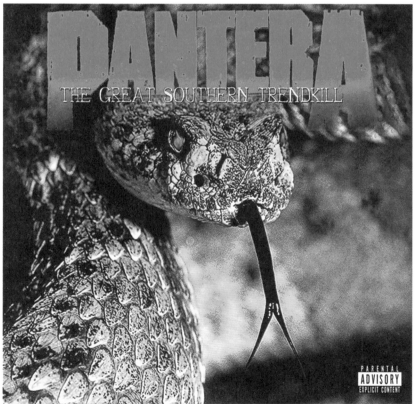

In the whole of classic literature, there are probably few works that have inspired this music and its graphic representations as much as John Milton's *Paradise Lost*. First published in 1667, it tells, in epic and romantic fashion, of the fall of Lucifer, God's favourite angel, who was expelled from Paradise for rebelling against the Almighty. The archetypal image of the so-called fallen angel was immortalized by Gustave Doré, and that engraving appears as a recurring motif in the visuals of **Lucifer's Fall** and **Regarde les hommes tomber**

(Watch Humanity Fall). Accompanied by other fallen angels, Lucifer departs, to go and hide in the bowels of the Earth, where he settles in the capital of Hell: Pandemonium, the abode of all demons. The best-known depictions of this infernal place are those by the painter John Martin. The most famous is in the Louvre Museum, and it appears on countless album sleeves. A rebellious angel who opposes God and forms an army of demons is an ideal metaphor for bands that seek to bring people together around music that is as violent and abrasive as the flames of Hell. Indeed, at the height of the Satanic Panic – the period between 1980 and 1990 during which American society saw the devil everywhere, most notably in rock and roll – there was a rumour that the name **KISS** stood for 'Knights in Satan's Service', doubtless a reference to Pandemonium, Lucifer and the legions that served him. But beyond these rumours, which served the purposes of the sanctimonious as much as the marketing of bands, there is, in the fate of Lucifer and the depictions of Paradise, an immense wealth of dark fantasy, a Dantesque, romantic aesthetic: the story of a misunderstood angel who seeks revenge on a blind God. Milton's work has been a key inspiration for many paintings of Hell, along with Dante's *Divine Comedy*. Of course, these works came much later than the Bible, but they led to the first noteworthy representations of Hell. These two literary works were foundation stones for all the sombre art that was to follow them – and, without a doubt, constitute two of the pillars upon which the metal aesthetic rests.

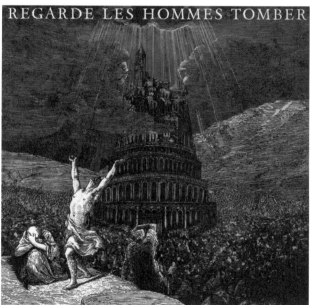

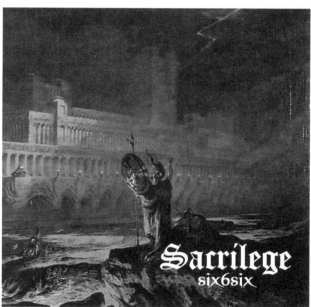

Goat Bong – *Entranced by Sound & Smoke*

Lucifer's Fall – *Lucifer's Fall*

Regarde les hommes tomber – *Regarde les hommes tomber*

Sacrilege – *Six6Six*

Rather like Lucifer, whose Latin name means 'light-bearer', Prometheus is, in Greek mythology, the transmitter of fire, who stole the sacred fire from the gods of Olympus to give it to humans. This element thus symbolizes the almost technological evolutionary leap of humankind. With fire came civilization. As is often the case with symbols, fire is highly ambivalent, being the bringer of both death and development. It is the primordial element: it creates the heat at the heart of the planets, and is what awaits us in the depths of Hell. This mythical aspect of fire is perfectly portrayed on the sleeves of the albums *Of Fire and Stars* by **Desert Near the End** and *Firestorm* by **Ambush**. One of the four elements of the alchemic sciences, fire is also a symbol of worship and adoration. *Ascension*, by the group **Regarde les hommes tomber**, depicts worshippers prostrating themselves around the sacred fire to invoke dark cosmic entities. But, as portrayed on *Fatal Portrait* by **King Diamond**, fire was also used to burn witches, so strong was the belief in the expiatory virtue of the flames, which were alone believed capable of destroying their so-called sin. With its links to humankind and its violence, fire can, unsurprisingly, show itself to be murderous and dangerous when it suits the needs of warfare – something perfectly symbolized on the sleeve of *Hellfire*, by the group **1349**, with its image of a knight's helmet licked by flames. The whole vocabulary of fire reeks of destruction, Hell and warfare: wildfires, flames, hot coals, pyres, sparks, explosions and more. Metal formed an association with it early on, if only as a form of theatre. Countless groups use pyrotechnics to create an infernal atmosphere at concerts, and this was elevated to an art form by the German group **Rammstein**. The pioneer in this area was **Arthur Brown**: not content with being the inventor of corpse paint, he was one of  the first to use fire as a prop – during a performance of his song 'Fire'. On album covers, fire has become even more common. On *Branded and Exiled* by **Running Wild**, flames turn the pentagram branding iron red. On *Fireball* by **Deep Purple** the band themselves appear, dreamlike, in a ball of fire: a comet in musical space. Although it is not always in the foreground, the orange-red colour of fire is often present, as if this palette were, by definition, essential to a musical genre that aims to appear volcanic and abrasive. Everything that constitutes menace tinged with fascination can be found in metal, and fire is doubtless its most ancestral incarnation.

Desert Near the End – *Of Fire and Stars*
Rammstein – *Live Aus Berlin*
Running Wild – *Branded and Exiled*

Although the 1960s and 1970s saw a certain amount of fantasy surrounding LSD, it was not the only psychotropic drug that artists of the time claimed to use and even glorified. Glancing at the sleeve of *Just a Poke* by **Sweet Smoke**, and listening briefly to its contents, is enough to realize that. Cannabis, as a fully fledged member of the group, has woven its way into stoner rock and, indeed, stoner doom. **Electric Wizard**, **Bongzilla**, and **Weedeater** offer musical Masses in which cannabis, among other substances, is part of the ritual of trance. The groups that claim they take drugs extol their direct effects and creative benefits, even creating musical subcategories directly connected to the consumption of substances, such as acid rock. These subcategories, devised by the children of rock, are well known for improvisation and a high degree of artistic disinhibition. The promotion of psychotropic drugs – aside from their recreational aspect – has the added advantage of being brazenly against the law and upsetting the established order of the most reactionary fringes of society. Drug use goes against widely accepted morals, and highlights the idea of being an outcast, on the sidelines. The kind of drugs used by artists has even been a decisive factor in the career of certain groups. A perfect example is **Lemmy Kilmister**, who in 1975 was thrown out of **Hawkwind** following his arrest for possession of drugs, but also because of his taste for amphetamines rather than other drugs seen as 'trippy'. His was a different kind of trip, which was all the more evident in light of the group he founded immediately afterwards – the much more vigorous, hyper and savage **Motörhead**! In a different genre, the mechanical, stimulating sounds of industrial post-punk music are often associated with psychotropic drugs and amphetamines. **Al Jourgensen** of the group **Ministry** lived up to these clichés. The singer was known for his health problems and run-ins with the law as a result of his excessive use of heroin and cocaine. **Nikki Sixx** of **Mötley Crüe** even laughed at his excesses

in his biography, and in the evocative song 'Kickstart My Heart'. Indeed, following a heroin overdose, the bassist was pronounced dead, and was then resuscitated immediately afterwards. As a final example, we could mention the famous song 'Master of Puppets' by **Metallica**, in which **James Hetfield** relates how drugs can exert a fiendish hold on a human being. What goes up must come down – and once the euphoria has passed, drugs always return to remind us of the other side of that particular coin.

Ministry – *From Beer to Eternamix*
Destruction – *Cracked Brain*
Electric Wizard – *Dopethrone*

One of the figures most widely quoted by the press in the days following the biggest metal festivals is the number of litres of beer sold, because of the sheer excess. Concert and festival culture is deeply ingrained among metal enthusiasts, and it is hard to forget that image of people boozing, so common is drunken behaviour at such gatherings. While this is true of the audience, it is also true of certain artists who, when on tour, may live a festive lifestyle every day, enjoying an endless party. The biographies of the most outrageously provocative groups often contain colourful stories about life on tour. Like drugs, alcohol can be involved in the development of a sound. **Lemmy Kilmister** was known for accompanying his daily doses of speed with whisky. The nonchalant riffs of **Type O Negative** would be far less intoxicating with a sober **Peter Steele**. The Dutch troubadours **Urfaust** draw their befuddled sound from an almost mystical drunkenness, seen in the image on the sleeve of their album *Trúbadóiri Ólta an Diabhail*, which depicts skeletons surrounded by bottles, one pounding on barrels as if on a drum kit. As for the world of the German band **Tankard**, it is a vibrant homage to beer and, through it, to a drunken, wild lifestyle, often indulged in by a whole fringe of the thrash metal scene. Dead bodies (and dead bottles) littering the floor, party scenes, a mascot brandishing a can… The sleeve of their album *The Morning After* depicts a metal fan waking up half drunk in a filthy apartment strewn with empty bottles. Although this vignette is not glorious, it is nevertheless presented here with a kind of tenderness towards young people, who, according to them, have a need for euphoria and intensity, even if it means paying the price upon waking. These artworks often speak for themselves, and the examples are legion. Sometimes they show the faint ridiculousness of the thirsty barbarian, as in the image on 'Vodka' by **Korpiklaani**. Metal has a special relationship with alcohol, and unsurprisingly the most common piece of merchandising that bands offer – after a T-shirt – is beer or wine in bottles bearing an image of the group in question. The straight edge movement – which rejects all drugs and sprang from youth crew hardcore punk – had trouble finding a way through such practices, despite the fact that hardcore and metal are intertwined in numerous ways.

Urfaust – *Trúbadóiri Ólta an Diabhail (Drunken Troubadour of the Devil)*
Tankard – *The Mourning After*
Tankard – *Beast of Bourbon*

Trúbadóirí Ólta an Diabhail

Sex before marriage, pornography and all other forms of unrestrained sexuality are, in the eyes of God, acts that distance us from what is good – and are often pointed at as being immoral. Ever since the biblical episode of Sodom and Gomorrah, sexual freedom and fornication, when not simply for the purpose of procreation, have been branded dirty and deviant. The cardinal sins, invented in the Middle Ages, designated lust as one of the seven deadly sins. The lifestyle of the clergy bore witness to this, with chastity being observed by those who offered their lives to God. Sexual pleasure doubtless comes too close to human desire and turns someone away from divine love. Taking a purely heterodox approach, certain black metal groups have offered visuals depicting the dirty, deviant aspect of taboo sex – and if religious symbols could be intermingled with these images of debauchery, so much the better. **Sarcófago** even went so far as to depict Death and Jesus kissing each other sensually. Sex viewed as a mystical offering to the devil is also a recurrent image in these artworks, as on the album *Witchcraft of Domination* by **Mørknatt**; these orgies are sometimes tinged with sadomasochism, as in the case of **Impure Essence**, **Marduk** and **Belphegor**. Often, bad taste rears its ugly head, as in the case of **Sextrash** with the visual for *Sexual Carnage*. And the most morbid and excessive groups, such as **Fornicator** and **Urgehal**, even go to the extent of depicting sexual violence on their album sleeves and describing it in their lyrics, with the aim of pushing boundaries around common values and shocking people beyond a purely religious perspective. It is also worth mentioning goregrind, a noise metal or groove metal – sometimes both – offshoot of the musical subgenre grindcore, which has a sub-branch of its own known as pornogrind. The themes it deals with and the visuals that accompany this music are exclusively pornographic in character. The album sleeves bear deviant, hardcore pornographic drawings, photos or video stills. Examples among the less hardcore include the French band **Gronibard**, while on a more 'hentai' trip there is **Jig-Ai**. These reach the extremes of a puerile, abstruse form of punk, with some groups deliberately going off-limits: their albums are not found in record shops and are banned by magazines, so hard to stomach are the visuals that accompany them.

"THEIR ALBUMS ARE NOT FOUND IN
RECORD SHOPS AND ARE BANNED
BY MAGAZINES, SO HARD TO
STOMACH ARE THE VISUALS THAT
ACCOMPANY THEM."

White sheep among the black sheep… there is a significant number of avowedly Christian bands in almost every genre of metal. Since the 1960s, there have been traces of Christianity in rock, as certain hippies joined American evangelical movements while continuing to play the same music. Others, such as **Larry Norman**, made a career out of the industry, even though they had the same Christian education as their parents. Some consider his first solo album, *Upon This Rock*, released in December 1969, to be the first Christian rock album. A whole trend followed during the 1970s, with groups such as **Resurrection Band** and the Swedish **Jerusalem**. The period produced interesting groups, such as **Agape**, who blended psychedelic-sounding rock with gospel. The 1980s saw their own pioneering groups: first and foremost **Stryper**, closely followed by **Leviticus**, **Angelica** and **Warlord**. The relationship with faith is sometimes made explicit; in other cases it is more insidious, with lyrics containing allegories or historical accounts. During the 1990s and 2000s, the word of the Lord continued to be spread through power metal groups such as **Narnia** and **Divinefire**. **Cesare Bonizzi**, a member of the Order of Friars Minor Capuchin in Milan, even ended up singing on the album *Droghe* (Drugs) by the group **Metalluminium**. The Italians renamed themselves **Fratello Metallo** (Brother Metal) in 2002, and until 2010 had the friar as their leader. They released an album and an EP, and gave several concerts, including one at Gods of Metal, the largest Italian festival of the genre. With their triumphant chord sequences, lyrics singing the praises of the Lord, and infectious enthusiasm, Christian heavy metal and power metal groups, describing themselves as 'white metal' in some cases, almost managed to create in audiences that visionary trance that occurs in some evangelical gatherings. Visually, the icon of an angel was very prominent, but none of these groups abused an ostentatious symbol to assert their identity. There

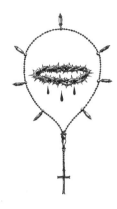

were unexpected Christian exponents of other genres too, such as thrash metal (**Tourniquet**), death metal (**Mortification**), nu metal (**POD**), and even black metal (**Horde**), which can sound discordant at first. The 2000s saw the birth of Christian hardcore, a heading under which come all metal groups with a hardcore punk streak and who openly acknowledged their spirituality in their lyrics. Some, such as **As I Lay Dying** and **August Burns Red**, achieved international success.

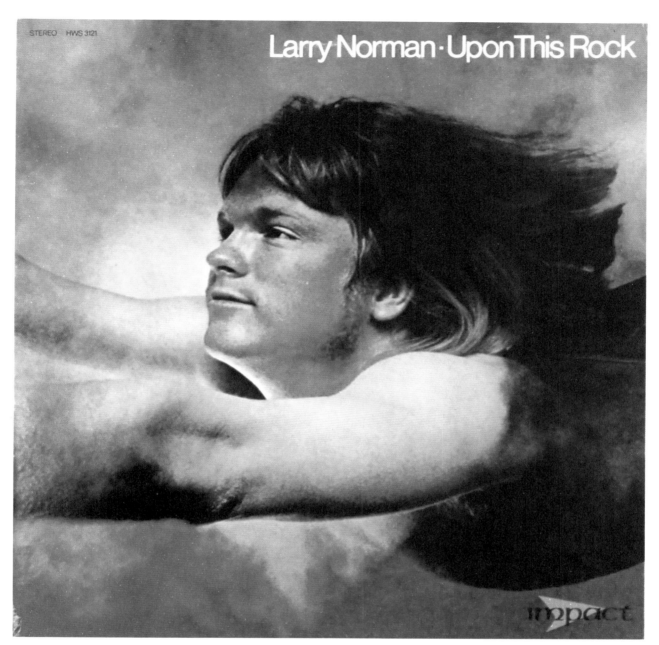

Larry Norman – *Upon This Rock*
Angelica – *Walkin' in Faith*
Divinefire – *Into a New Dimension*

MORES SILVAE

THE TRADITIONS
OF THE FOREST

If there is any place where mystery hides, out of sight and as close as possible to the wild world, it is the heart of the forest. In the collective imagination, it is here that secret meetings and witches' covens are held, where the strangest beasts lurk, and the spirits of nature lie dormant. The forest creates myths and legends by its very form: that of a labyrinth with endless paths, which symbolizes, par excellence, losing one's bearings. It is the perfect setting for stories and tales from a large number of cultures. Forests are home to ancient myths and magical creatures. In power metal, the forest is an ordeal that must be survived; it emanates a palpable magic, and is where fantastic creatures such as unicorns, elves, trolls and centaurs swarm. It symbolizes impenetrability, immutability, something that is hidden. In literature, trees sometimes even come to life, be it in Dante's *Divine Comedy* or the ents in Tolkien's *Lord of the Rings* – two works that have copiously fed the imaginary world of dark music. By contrast, in black metal, the approach is more pragmatic: the forest is portrayed in a much darker light. It is a dense, wooded mass – cold, wild and hostile. Most second-generation black metal groups

have posed in Nordic forests for music videos or promotional photographs. The forest can suggest an ancestral, often pagan, heritage. It is the silent, primitive witness to a bygone time, as in the case of **Drudkh**, who have adorned almost all their albums with images of inhospitable forests. **Striborg** have done likewise, placing the forest as the central element of their work. In depressive, suicidal black metal, the image of the forest is darker still, for it embodies the place of absolute solitude, far from human beings, where the misanthrope, wearied by the hubbub of the city, goes to try and disappear, rather like the hermit who retreats to the heart of the forest in order to make contact with the gods. It is the forest of 'Hop-o'-My-Thumb', where children are abandoned. The forest, thousands of years old, is a place of rest – sometimes even eternal rest. It represents a final destination where a human being decides of their own accord to return definitively to nature.

Striborg – *In the Heart of the Rainforest*
After Death Alone – *Suicide Forest* (demo, 2016)
Drudkh – *Forgotten Legends*
Elvenking – *Wyrd*

The wolf that howls in the night, chilling the blood of the disorientated traveller or the lost sheep, is one of the most ancestral images of fear. It is recurrent in the iconography of metal, often embodying nature and its laws, but possesses two distinct facets. The wolf is actually a timid creature, part of a social species that lives in packs, reflecting values linked to obedience and mutual assistance. However, stories and myths have often portrayed it as a solitary animal, aggressive and even bloodthirsty. An object of real fear in former times, the wolf gets a bad press even today. Several anecdotes of people being attacked by a wolf made the Beast of Gévaudan a firmly rooted part of French folklore. The wolf has been wrongly accused, hunted and endangered. It is an animal that is permanently misunderstood, and seems to be the perfect incarnation of an artist who identifies with these attributes. The howl of the wolf evokes the forest and nights of the full moon, scenes that feature in the visuals of old hard rock albums such as *Edge of the World* by the British band **Wolf**. In thrash metal and death metal, the wolf may take on a fantastic and aggressive appearance, whereas for bands such as the Finnish **Sonata Arctica**, it is a reassuring, loyal figure. **Catamenia**, another Finnish band, use it as a totem. Incidentally, the symbolism of the wolf had such an influence on black metal that **Kristian Vikernes**, of the one-man band **Burzum**, used **Varg** as a pseudonym – *Varg* meaning 'wolf' in Old Norse. Both *varg* and 'wolf' feature in the names of many (often black metal) groups. The wolf is a charismatic, multiform creature that musicians adapt according to the feelings they wish to convey. The analogy between humans and wolves is always very prominent in lyrics, as if it is the animal that is most emblematic of the solitary,

self-sufficient wanderer. Odin himself was accompanied by two mythical wolves, Geri and Freki. Finally, the mythical figure of the werewolf, symbol of transformation and mutation, exploits the wild character of the wolf, which cannot be tamed – the emblem of a return to the wild state. Adopting a more B-movie approach, the group **Powerwolf** even made it their official mascot.

Catamenia – *Eternal Winter's Prophecy*
Toxic Holocaust – *An Overdose of Death*
Legion of the Damned – *Sons of the Jackal*

Let us leave the forest behind, and rise above it. The forest – of which we can now see only the canopy – is just a minute part of those wild expanses you can find in a landscape. Only nature untouched by humans has this power to enthral us with its overwhelming immensity. Numerous pagan folk metal groups, atmospheric black metal groups, and other sub-branches of metal seeking to make the Earth's vibrations resonate have drawn on these panoramas. Moving and terrible landscapes adorn their album sleeves, which doubtless explains why several dozen groups have used works by Caspar David Friedrich, the painter who is most emblematic of German Romanticism. In these landscapes, everything is magnified – human beings are tiny, almost invisible, and from a distance everything becomes smooth and perfect. From afar, an uncultivated field is a unified, green expanse. This sense of dizziness can be found in all landscapes. From the majestic fjords of **Windir** and **Enslaved** to the infinite valleys of **Winterfylleth** and **Blut Aus Nord**; from the blueish expanses of water of **Falkenbach** and **Eldamar** to the reddening skies of **Bathory** and **Nokturnal Mortum**, numerous artists have chosen these

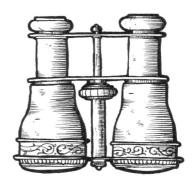

melancholy, peaceful visions to illustrate their music, inviting the listener to put themselves in the place of Friedrich's famous traveller who, from the top of a mountain, contemplates a sea of cloud. Such landscapes accompany vast, deep music, whose sound encourages contemplation. With some groups, it is not even clear whether these backdrops are real or unreal, whether they depict an existing place or are born of some marvellous world. Sometimes reflections of light, the colours of an image's elements, or a ruin with improbably fantastic architecture indicate that this is a fantasy world, when this is not taken for granted as it is with **Sojourner** and **Cân Bardd**. Going even further, the group **Summoning** frame their visuals in order to make the featured panoramas of Middle-earth sublime, as if viewed from the window of a castle. The dungeon synth musical style (of which **Summoning** are exponents) is a dreamlike offshoot of black metal in which the synthesizer is predominant, often even being the only instrument. The style began in the 1990s and saw a wave of popularity during the 2010s; these visuals became one of the recurrent codes of the genre. Often performed by a single, generally anonymous musician, dungeon synth music is always shrouded in an aura of mystery. For this reason, dungeon synth often comes in the form of a cassette. To offer, today, an obsolete medium, like a small artefact dug out from the back of a cupboard, is to adopt a backward-looking, nostalgic approach. A cassette of dungeon synth music is a small window into a marvellous world: an old-fashioned postcard sent from the other side, inviting us on a journey.

Enslaved – *Frost*

Bathory – *Twilight of the Gods*

Eldamar – *The Force of the Ancient Land*

Windir – *Likferd*

When winter arrives and the world goes to sleep, covered in a white mantle, a sort of muffled silence descends… Time seems to stop – to the point that snow symbolizes glacial cold and death. One could remain frozen in it forever. When snow is swept along by the wind or avalanches, it can turn violent and make us disappear, like a sandstorm in the desert. Soothing and yet fatal, it is a perfect symbol for the eternal, misanthropic coldness of black metal. However, beneath its apparent homogeneity it conceals an especially magnificent fractal crystalline structure. It is thus an ideal substance when the aim is to highlight purity, complexity and death. One dreadful story – among many others – features in the history of Norwegian black metal. It involves the group **Windir**, whose leader, **Valfar**, was found frozen to death in the valley of Sogndal on 17 January 2004, at the age of just 25. An autopsy showed he had died of hypothermia. This story reflects a whole state of mind peculiar to Nordic black metal. Northern peoples know very well that a blizzard is one of the cruellest and most pitiless kinds of bad weather. A whole vocabulary revolving around cold and ice has evolved in the world of black metal, with these conditions leaving their mark on significant albums such as *Blizzard Beasts* and *At the Heart of Winter* by **Immortal**. Moreover, the group went on to popularize this adoration for snow and frozen environments in black metal. Cold does not only come from outside: in black metal, it is common to put on a mask of indifference, like an outer skin worn by the artist that places a wall of ice between them and the rest of the world, allowing no glimpse of any joyous emotion - as if the soul were frozen solid in the ice. This can give give a misanthropic aura to a musical style that claims to hate conformism and

narrow-mindedness. Some melodic metal groups close to power metal and melodic speed also like to heighten ideas related to the winter season in a more cheerful vein. **Sonata Arctica** and **Wintersun**, to name just the two best-known, take us back to Christmas stories and the magic of snow-covered landscapes.

Immortal – *At the Heart of Winter*
Windir – *1184*

The sun always sinks eventually. All journeys end in dark night. While it is the temple of darkness, wild beasts and criminals, night is also the only time we can see the stars of our galaxy. The spectacle of daylight is extinguished, giving way to its dark side. Night is silent, and deprives us of sight. It has been a threat to humans for so long that we have retained a certain fear of it, and we associate it with particular folk tales. It symbolizes the approach of old age and death, but also mystery and creation. Night conceals the real world, and offers the artist a blank page to create – as if, against this nocturnal backdrop, the imagination can take its rightful place more easily. Synonymous with the end of the world, but also with its beginning, the night before the dawn of time carries a heavy, macabre symbolism. It is the daughter of darkness, and embodies the death of the sun. A setting for the paranormal and for revelations, night is also the time of nightmares and of the unconscious: from there, monsters emerge. It can be the night of the living dead, the night of the hunter, the night through which danger comes forth. As it did with snow, black metal made night its ally, and it features on a number of cult

album sleeves. The most emblematic is probably that of *A Blaze in the Northern Sky* by **Darkthrone**, with its screaming face covered in corpse paint springing forth from the darkness. In black metal, a style of music that shares the colour of night, there is a resigned determinism; and, rather than be afraid of this darkness, some set out to tame it. That is when black metal becomes an ode to the night, to the absence of colour. More generally, the aesthetic and symbolism of night have inspired a substantial number of groups, with the word featuring in the names of hundreds of bands, and at least as many album titles. Darkness is a common trait in a whole swathe of metal. While black metal has made it its leitmotif, the call of the void, the advance towards a cold, deep abyss is inextricably linked to many sub-branches of this genre, with the most extreme being most heavily involved.

Nuit Noire – *Lunar Deflagration*
Emperor – *In the Nightside Eclipse*

Hellhammer, the youthful first version of the great **Celtic Frost**, were inspired by the 'do it yourself' photocopied aesthetic of punk to create their black and white imagery. Dark and extreme visuals dealing with sinister themes were subsequently among the predominant influences on the metal movement. Symbolic of a duality that is both conflicting and complementary, black and white can be seen in a large number of these visuals. This polarization embodies the balance of values and equilibrium. Light and dark, night and day, truth and lies, good and evil. Using black and white means choosing to be direct and definite. Colour is useless compared to the clarity of the message and intention of a black-and-white image – and metal clearly claimed the darker of the two. It is the black stain on the white cloth of purity and innocence. So, in the 1990s, a white face on a black background certainly became black metal's most recurrent visual. At the start of the 1980s, although still remaining heavy metal, **Mercyful Fate**, with **King Diamond** as leader, became the first group to make black and white make-up their trademark. Looking further into the history of this macabre make-up, **Arthur Brown** used it in 1968 in the video for the song

'Fire'. But that was not what drove the Norwegian pioneers to use these masks of paint, though it inevitably had an impact. Sometimes called 'war paint', referencing warriors' use of body paint to intimidate their enemies, this make-up, which became a tradition, reflected a desire to be dehumanized and resemble death. **Mayhem**, the first Norwegian black metal group, drew heavily on the Brazilian band **Sarcófago** for their aesthetic, and today a plethora of ghosts appear on gloomy monochrome images.

Hellhammer – *Triumph of Death*
King Diamond – *Conspiracy*
Immortal – *Pure Holocaust*

RITUS MORTE

RITUALS OF DEATH

The Grim Reaper is the most widespread personification of death in Western culture. This deathly, indeed skeletal figure is the harbinger of the imminent death of the person it is visiting. Although sometimes it acts as a guide in the passage from one world to the next, most often it comes to blindly harvest the souls of the living and lead them to their deaths. This is why it is most often depicted carrying a scythe – except that this is used not to mow grain, but to harvest our lives. Depictions of the Reaper often appear in fantastic engravings supposedly illustrating periods of devastating plague. Death is such a real presence in all cultures that it is not surprising it has been personified, even though it has been given the appearance of a collection of bones devoid of all living substance. This vision has become iconic, to the point of sometimes becoming a cliché. The albums by the group **Grim Reaper** have exploited this figure in all its emblematic forms: riding a black stallion and brandishing its scythe against a gloomy sky, standing in a cemetery, leaning over a dying knight, and even bursting through a church's stained-glass window at the wheel of a powerful car. In less flamboyant fashion, the Reaper appears on every one of the albums by **Children of Bodom**, so has become an essential hallmark of theirs. However, despite their originality in depicting the Reaper with a human face, the rendering is closer to a failed cosplay than it is to a terrifying image. The highly cultish group **Black Sabbath** also had their 'Reaper' phase during the 1990s with the album *Dehumanizer*, followed three years later by *Forbidden*, whose sleeves show death incarnate with its merciless scythe. A group that highlights this symbol certainly aims to demonstrate the darkness of their ideology and aesthetic, but also aims to embrace death, make it their own, almost make a friend of it. The music the depiction heralds echoes its image: merciless,

mystical, macabre and legendary… in a word, deathly. The Reaper as a horseman of the Apocalypse appears on the sleeves of **Blue Öyster Cult** and **Grave Digger**, and it will be interesting to see whether this representation will continue over the centuries. In any event, in the metal aesthetic, the Reaper has found a setting that was eager to receive it.

Blue Öyster Cult – *Some Enchanted Evening*
Grim Reaper – *See You in Hell*
Children of Bodom – *Follow the Reaper*

SKULLS

In the spirit of the black pirate flag, announcing plunder and destruction, the skull is an archetypal image. The group **Misfits**, the highly influential face of horror punk started by **Glenn Danzig** in 1977, made it their emblem. It figured in their stage make-up, but also on their famous logo. Their mascot, The Fiend – for it has a name – is drawn directly from the American serial *Crimson Ghost*, released in 1946, which follows the machinations of a caped criminal who hides behind a skeleton disguise. Although the singer and performer **Screamin' Jay Hawkins** was already in the habit of posing with human skulls during his performances in the 1950s, it was heavy metal that really developed this theme. *The Dungeons are Calling* by **Savatage** and *Fire in the Brain* by **Oz** both had the distinctive feature of using veritable photographic compositions as artwork. The hyperrealistic quality obtained by using a real photograph is destabilizing. A direct descendant of the *vanitas* still lifes of the 16th and 17th centuries, the skull is often accompanied by a whole convention that is supposed to sustain a metaphor. *Self-Extinction* by **Inhumankind** pays perfect homage to this vision of vanity. In other cases, several skulls are piled up together in sinister heaps. Extreme metal often invites us to look into the tomb, to succumb to our fascination for the clammy, deathly aesthetic given off by the charnel house and the mass grave. This catacomb-like aura is showcased by **Disma** on their EP *The Graveless Remains*. The skull is the perfect totem for a dark death metal, with elephantine rhythms and guitars with drop tuning. Also worthy of note is the corpse paint used by black metal bands, which sometimes imitates the shape of a human skull – again, with the aim of personifying death. In a style that is closer to that of comics, **Megadeth** featured the skeleton Vic Rattlehead. Several groups appropriated this

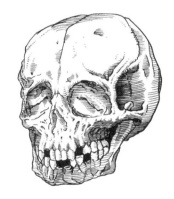

iconography, which has almost become a cliché, but only the group **Satan** managed to render the skull almost divine with a style reminiscent of classical painting. The genre did not confine itself to representations of human skulls. Snaggletooth, the skull that appears on most **Motörhead** sleeves, resembles that of a wild boar, and **Job for a Cowboy** have as their mascot a strange recurring character with a buffalo skull in place of a face. Although it is an image of a head stripped of its flesh, the skull nevertheless possesses a life of its own – one that metal has resolutely revived. From the biker to the hoodlum, it is the ultimate emblem of those who cheat death.

Disma – *The Graveless Remains*
Oz – *Fire in the Brain*

ZOMBIES

The original zombie was far from the one that prowls our imagination today. The group **White Zombie**, through its name, incidentally paid homage to the eponymous movie, released in 1932 and featuring one of the first stars of horror films, Bela Lugosi. Originating in voodooism, the zombie was the victim of mental enslavement, closer to spirit possession than to the brain-eating living dead that we know today. Only the expressionless, empty gaze of a figure deprived of its humanity has been retained. It was through George Romero and his *Night of the Living Dead* saga that the zombie attained its modern form, much broader in its symbolism, which metal instinctively adopted. The zombie can also symbolize overconsumption, war and its victims, the spread of a virus, a social revolt, or even an image of the Apocalypse. In the artwork for *Hell on Earth*, **Toxic Holocaust** display ordinary humans transformed into crazed zombies that wander through the ruins of destroyed civilization. The album's title pays homage to Romero's movies: 'When there's no more room in Hell, the dead will walk the earth.' They are the army of the end of time, the final stage of a humanity that has ended up becoming rotten and devouring itself. **Aborted** take an even more infernal approach with *TerrorVision*, depicting zombies impaled on the claws of demons that make them walk forwards like puppets. Although the almost gothic vision of the living dead emerging from the grave was employed by **Necrophagia**, **Mortician**, **Lordi** and **Death**, metal generally presents a gorier vision of the zombie that is completely uninhibited, closer to the grisly *Crossed* comics by Garth Ennis than it is to *The Walking Dead*. On *Hordes of Zombies* by **Terrorizer**, the living dead are not empty shells seeking nourishment but terrifying hordes with malevolent eyes, within which punks and ecclesiastics march towards us with the same noxious look. The group deliver an incisive death metal, as unstoppable as the army of living dead that they display on their album sleeve. With **Zombie Riot**, the zombie replaces the hero, who, in a spirit of protest, announces the raising of a ghostly army. Here, the zombie is the outcast, forgotten, cursed – an idea explored in Romero's *Land of the Dead*. The title of the **Zombie Riot** album *Reign of Rotten Flesh* says a lot about the symbolic power the zombie can embody, if only because of the eternal degradation it represents. Rottenness and death rise up – and this music is their war cry.

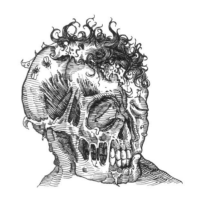

Terrorizer – *Hordes of Zombies*
Toxic Holocaust – *Hell on Earth*
Zombie Riot – *Reign of Rotten Flesh*

TERRORIZER
HORDES OF ZOMBIES

HELL ON EARTH

BODY HORROR

Rejected from the start by all kinds of moralizing right thinking, metal naturally developed in an atmosphere of excess, brandished as a form of freedom. The rhythmic, symbolic violence of extreme music calls for visuals that leave a mark… or that shock. From the mid-1980s, groups with evocative names began to appear: **Possessed**, **Death**, **Cannibal Corpse**, **Autopsy**, **Napalm Death**, **Repulsion**, **Terrorizer** and others. These were the new groups of a metal scene that was constantly evolving, in the grip of a permanent raising of the stakes. The thrash metal of the early 1980s slowly began to give way to death metal and grindcore, with bands that – by virtue of their sound, their concepts and their visuals – pushed the limits further still. Some of the typefaces used in logos evoked bodily fluids or decomposing flesh, and the atrocities that appeared on album sleeves left no doubt as to the musicians' graphic influences. Skulls, mutilated bodies that were decomposing or mutating, zombies walking off in tatters… Many of these groups were raised on the gore exploitation movies of the 1970s and 1980s. For example, something of the repellent ending of Brian Yuzna's movie *Society* appears in the artwork on *An Epiphany of Hate* by the group **Master**, with those faces stuck together. While the first sleeves in the style were more reminiscent of inoffensive little drawings by teenagers fascinated by the culture of alternative cinema, talented illustrators would seize upon album sleeves in a much more serious way, to show scenes that were ever more gory, and also, in the case of certain grindgore groups, with rather more assertive political resonance. The decomposition of bodies and our relationship with our own decay are leading themes of the genre, as demonstrated by the design of the album *Slowly We Rot* by **Obituary**. Early explorations of body horror can be seen in the movies of David Cronenberg, from *The Fly* to

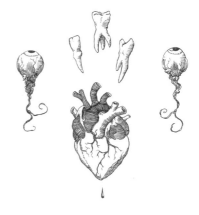

Videodrome. As the conversation around horror developed, the iconography of these groups evolved, improving with every album – as did their musical style, which was honed as time went on. Blast beats, growling sounds, ultra-saturated guitars, outrageous lyrics… death metal was to music what ultra-gore movies were to cinema. The implicit message conveyed by such visuals is that if you can bear such horrible images, you are capable of appreciating this type of extreme music. They acted almost as a warning.

Master – *An Epiphany of Hate*
Horrid – *Beyond the Dark Border*

MEDICINE

The artwork of *Reek of Putrefaction*, the first album by **Carcass**, released in 1988, is a patchwork of real photographs, particularly distressing to behold, which are all from medical textbooks. Burns, skin conditions, infections, buboes and blemishes... The entire spectrum of physical decay is contained in a single album sleeve, saturated and repellent, so much does it throw in our face something we want neither to see nor to experience. On *Surgical Steel*, the same group approaches the subject from the opposite direction, displaying all the surgeon's frightening instruments, to convey the coldness and precision of the person who is going to operate on you. This time the group relies on suggestion rather than disgust, but the intentions and effects are the same. While the medical world is first and foremost connected to healing, care and a form of altruistic goodness, there is a darker side to this vision. Indeed, a doctor is someone who faces the horror that only violence or illness can create. Present until a person's final moments, doctors are the living people who come into closest contact with death. It is hardly surprising, then, that some groups turned their attention to the tormented imagination of medicine to illustrate the deviant world they wanted to portray. There is always that small, frightened voice in the background when we entrust ourselves to a masked individual armed with a scalpel. We wonder whether the surgeon will really accomplish their task. What if they became mad, or negligent? Some groups have gone further, and transformed them into outright sadists. In the tradition of horror films such as *The Dentist* and

Dr. Giggles, **Autopsy** released an album cover for *Severed Survival* showing four zombie surgeons wielding scalpels; the way in which they are drawn creates the illusion that they are about to operate on the person looking at the sleeve, placing the viewer, against their will, in a position of submission. **Aborted** went further with a visual for the album *The Archaic Abattoir*: the doctor is a cross between Dexter and Leatherface, with whom he shares a love of chainsaw massacres. **Haemorrhage** had fun with symbols on *Apology for Pathology*, displaying a blood-red cross reminiscent of the one used to symbolise medical care, but which, on closer inspection, reveals disturbing gory images, melded with the red of the cross. Finally, **Holocausto Canibal** plays with the relative beauty of the body, so much studied by classical painters. Their album *Catalépsia Necrótica* calls to mind anatomical wax models and paintings from the time of the 16th-century French surgeon Ambroise Paré. This fascination with medicine is translated into music that is precise and sharp-edged, mortal and surgical.

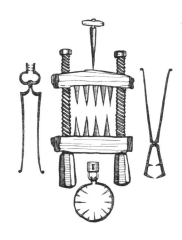

From a historical point of view, torture is associated with the Inquisition and similar kinds of obscurantism. The fate reserved for witches and heretics was so cruel and atrocious that it called into question the limits of our humanity and empathy. Christianity itself is symbolized by an instrument of torture – the cross – and at the heart of this religion is the sacrifice of Jesus, who endured crucifixion for the love of humankind. The full horror of such torture can be felt on the cover of *The Impious Doctrine* by **Carnivorous Voracity**. The emphasis is often on the martyrdom of the torture victim, who is punished as an example in front of terrified, excited crowds – something that is perfectly depicted by **Gutslit** in the artwork for *Amputheatre*. The torturer's kit consists of tools specifically designed to inflict suffering, which is itself instructive of the depths to which the human soul can sink. This is explored in a direct, medieval manner by **Brodequin** on *Instruments of Torture*, which shows the sheer horror of such practices. Torture is so morally unacceptable that the subject is inevitably exploited by a musical genre that explores the outer limits of the extreme. A saturated and extremely harsh guitar sound, sharp, rapid drumming that leaves very little room for silence, and vocals that are mostly screaming can seem like the perfect soundtrack to someone being 'put to the question' – another term for torture. The link between the music and the bloodstained images suggests that the contents of the album are a form of torture by sound: an auditory massacre. That rings all the more true given the fact that during the Iraq War, the US army played tracks by **Metallica** and **AC/DC** at very high volumes to torture prisoners. In a different context, that anecdote might raise a smile, for these groups are, after all, fairly accessible compared to much more extreme branches of metal. It was in the 1990s, when death metal was on the rise, that there began to be a proliferation of visuals depicting maltreatment of the human body. Whether torture is inflicted through sounds, or mentally or physically, the idea here is to depict the most dreadful, disturbing suffering, whether the group approaches it from the perspective of the victim or that of the torturer. The group **Cannibal Corpse** made a tradition of these visual codes, alternating between Z movies and obscurantism. Numerous groups have since displayed this type of iconography, to the point of no longer making these images as sensational as they should be, at least for devotees of the genre. Brutal death, deathgrind, and slam death metal are specialists of the discipline, featuring extremely graphic illustrations that are nevertheless very beautiful, very fine, and sometimes highly coloured. A certain sophistication in brutality is characteristic of these album covers, but despite that, they are very disconcerting to the novice.

Brodequin – *Instruments of Torture*

 **MADNESS**

Listening to 'Paranoid' by **Black Sabbath**, in which **Ozzy Osbourne** recounts what seems to come close to an episode of depression, is enough to realize that the subject of mental illness is omnipresent in metal. Just as bluesmen did before them, many rock, punk and metal artists have demonstrated insight into their own psychological issues, and shown themselves to be highly sensitive to the mental health of the world around them. While they did not all show this directly, the clearest traces of this suffering and their insight into it can be found in their music. Anxiety, paranoia, madness, the feeling of being marginalized by the system – all this can come through in songs, lyrics, voice texture and, above all, the aesthetic of the group and its artistic direction. The success encountered by some artists, and fantasies about their mental state, will perhaps even have tended to romanticize psychological problems, as if these were the expression of deliberate marginalization. And yet rock has seen some of its idols succumb to their mental health issues. After he was expelled from **Pink Floyd** because of his behaviour as a result of bipolar disorder, it was said of **Syd Barrett** that he was the greatest casualty in the history of rock. **New Order** was founded after the split of **Joy Division**, following the suicide of **Ian Curtis**, who was in a black hole, suffering a profound bout of depression. The arrival of extreme metal tended to put such illnesses under the spotlight. **Julien Truchan**, singer of the French death metal group **Benighted**, is a psychiatric nurse, which doubtless explains the padded cell on the cover of *ICP*. To write his lyrics, he draws inspiration from the patients he meets day to day. Contrary to what some of his group's artworks suggest, he approaches the subject from an angle different from that of horror films and the clichés that drive sufferers of mental health issues to exclusion from society. The

world of psychiatry as portrayed in thrash metal and death metal often conveys the hell of solitude, madness and chemical prisons – as is perfectly illustrated on the cover of *Schizophrenia* by **Sepultura**, and the prison-like aura of the album *Where Hatred Dwells and Darkness Reigns* by **Zornheym**. Depressive and suicidal black metal is a subgenre that also evokes psychiatric disorders, but seen from a more sombre, introspective point of view. Unsurprisingly, these are often one-man bands. The vocabulary of their lyrics revolves around suicide and darkness, reflecting a profound inner angst that is sometimes incurable. Here, too, there is a noticeable tendency to inappropriately aestheticize mental health problems – which, alas, sometimes verges on the pathetic.

EEN PATHOLOGIE VAN DE GENEESHEER

Hell's Domain – *Hell's Domain*
Psyche – *Een pathologie van de geneesheer* (A Pathology of the Physician)

CANNIBALISM

Similarly to horror films, metal has evolved by ceaselessly pushing back the boundaries of terror and shattering the frontiers of violence. In a sort of tacit crusade against convention, in law and in morals, death metal has not hesitated to explore one of the last taboos: cannibalism. This is where the line is often drawn between savagery and civilization, and it is certain that most of the groups that deal with this theme have seen the movie *Cannibal Holocaust* directed by Ruggero Deodato. In its day, this classic of gore shocked the entire world and created a subgenre in its own right, opening up a new era in the world of horror films. The American group **Impetigo** probably even based their visuals on Deodato's cult movie. Cannibalism is a bridge to all corners of the world of horror, from zombies to psychopaths. It is the metaphor for a humanity that devours itself, and for competitive violence among humans. **Cannibal Corpse** drew the first part of their name directly from the movie, and the group would be a major influence on the genre, popularizing atrocious scenes of zombified humans mutilating and devouring each other on their album covers. Man is wolf to man, and such a de facto taboo causes a sense of malaise in the listener that the music's violence only deepens. On their album *Cannibal*, **Wretched** even made this taboo 'industrial' by portraying a gigantic skull swallowing human heads laid on a conveyor belt – suggesting that society is, in fact, devouring itself. In speed metal and thrash metal, the idea of cannibalism is often used to depict a newly barbarous world where moral values have been annihilated following a collapse of civilization, always with that touch of futuristic anticipation peculiar to the genre. The subject is also dealt with by **Rammstein** in their song 'Mein Teil' (My Part), in which two men agree to eat each other – a reference to the Rotenburg Cannibal affair, a story that shook Germany in 2001. Some groups have tried to play

with the taboo in a humorous way, as in the case of **Devour the Fetus** with their artwork for *Cook'n'Roll*, in which the meat of a hamburger is replaced with foetuses, the whole image drawn in a style reminiscent of a comic strip. Curiously, metal is one of the few genres that lets such horrors pass without them being seen as especially shocking: horror and deviancy are its main foundation, and this raising of the stakes often signifies posturing or bravado rather than a real, sincere commendation of this gastronomic approach.

Rammstein – 'Mein Teil'
Impetigo – *Ultimo Mondo Cannibale* (Last Cannibal World)

GORE

The cover of *Symphonies of Sickness* by **Carcass** features a collage that is especially distressing to look at, for it consists of medical photographs of the symptoms of particularly awful illnesses, as well as corpses and autopsies. The album's very title makes it clear that the group's aesthetic revolves around the decay of bodies, suffering, and death. Directly descended from the first offerings from **Carcass**, a whole swathe of goregrind drew a line under the unrealistic, 'cartoonish' aspect of the first death metal album covers, opting instead for absolutely grisly photographs. More direct and disturbing than a drawing, these images from the darkest depths of the internet, or from forensic medicine files, automatically restrict these groups to the underground circuit. Beyond the desire to shock, the use of this artwork is also a way of placing themselves on the margins, showing that they have extricated themselves from the mainstream and from the media circus. The artists of the gore scene, who inherited the spirit of the website Rotten.com, pushed boundaries musically as well as visually. By mangling and twisting even more the typefaces of death metal logos – already barely legible to the uninitiated – and melding them with photographs of guts, rotting flesh and bodily fluids, they imposed on the viewer the worst possible view of human anatomy. All this was helped by technically poorly executed montages, coloured compositions and assertive minimalism. This approach gives a discomfortingly almost childlike appearance to these creations, which is in total contradiction with the forbidden, traumatizing images being shown. In goregrind, it is no longer a game – the aim is to make it as sordid, almost as inhuman, as possible. **Last Days of Humanity** provide a good example: the album artwork for *Putrefaction in Progress* features a close-up of a decomposing human body. As for the title of their second album – *The Sound of Rancid Juices Sloshing Around Your Coffin* – it describes perfectly the adventure in sound that awaits us. Goregrind vocals are indeed highly distinctive, resembling guttural, incomprehensible belching that plunges us into total malaise. This style aims to drag us into the depths of organic horror, with a certain nihilism that fits perfectly with the genre's deathly aesthetic. Goregrind takes a unique approach, which seems to do all it can to discourage us, but will, however, continue to attract some, by showing absolutely horrific visuals that no news programme, no matter how unprincipled, would dare show.

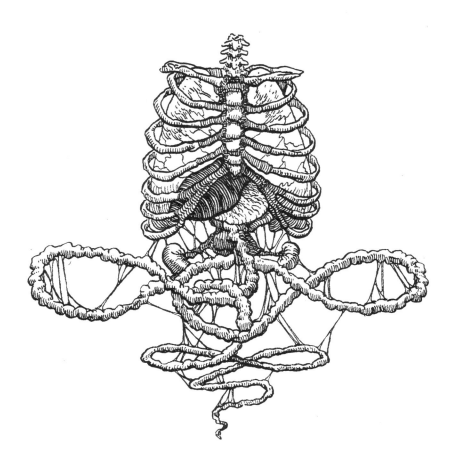

"THIS STYLE AIMS TO DRAG US
INTO THE DEPTHS OF ORGANIC
HORROR, WITH A CERTAIN NIHILISM
THAT FITS PERFECTLY WITH THE
GENRE'S DEATHLY AESTHETIC."

SUSURRUS

MURMURS FROM
THE DEPTHS

TENEBRARUM

FANTASTIC

Fantastic literature is regarded as having started in the late 18th century with the English gothic novel. Its protagonists are enveloped by Victorian interiors and a nebulous atmosphere, inside decrepit old castles, crypts or cemeteries, lit by chandeliers or the light of the moon: settings conducive to stories about murders, ghosts, vampires and exorcisms. **Jonas Åkerlund**, the Swedish director of the movie *Lords of Chaos* and music videos for Madonna, shot his first official audiovisual project in 1988. It was a video for 'Bewitched' by **Candlemass**. In it, **Messiah Marcolin**, the group's vocalist at the time, appears disguised as a monk-magician who has been brought back from the dead and casts a spell on his victims, with the aim of forming an army of zombies devoted to the cause of doom metal. The action takes place in an English-style landscaped park shrouded in a thick mist. It is partly a clumsy homage to horror films and partly a nod to the fantastic novel, and a similar quality can be found in all the branches of metal linked to gothic literature, such as epic doom metal, black metal and, indeed, gothic metal. Album covers regularly immerse the viewer in settings that are carved out of rock and imbued with a dark romanticism; for example, in the case of **Opeth**'s *In Cauda Venenum*, this takes the form of a gothic manor house. In the foreground, a horse-drawn carriage, doubtless the one that will take the listener to the heart of the album, has just been parked in front of the building; from every lit window of the latter, a frightening figure stares out, as if expecting you. There is no monster or anything supernatural, yet the image is suffused with strange, fantastic atmosphere. Depending on the artist and the approach taken, styles vary, even to the point of sometimes falling into cliché: the album *The 13th Floor* by **Sirenia** depicts the white figure of a lady in a gothic corridor who is about to step on the number 13, which is filled with fantastic connotations in our collective imagination. The outfits worn often look incongruous because of their dark classicism, as in the case of the Swedish group **Tribulation**,

who look as if they just stepped out of a Tim Burton movie. The lyrics, if we focus on the most passionate, contain real, little storylines – dark, poetic tales and fables, sometimes accompanied by the traditional fantastic bestiary. That is the case with the concept album *Carpathia: A Dramatic Poem* by **The Vision Bleak**, which conjures up the fantasy of the Carpathian Mountains and the vampire myths associated with them. The fantastic is sometimes more existential and modern, as in the case of *Climbin' the Walls* by **Wrathchild America**, which shows a figure caught in a satanic labyrinth that is strongly reminiscent of the maze of Leviathan dreamed up by Clive Barker in his masterpiece *Hellraiser*.

Hagzissa – *They Ride Along*
The Vision Bleak – *Carpathia: A Dramatic Poem*

 **DREAD**

The fantastic genre is characterized by the sense of gnawing dread that it gives off when its heroes experience the worrying strangeness of a reality that is becoming clouded. The protagonist of a fantastic novel is always faced with fear, madness, the inexplicable and the forces of the paranormal. This approach leaves the reader floating weightlessly in a space filled with doubt, without really being able to tell truth from falsehood. Edgar Allan Poe was one of the genre's pioneers, and his works influenced many that followed, ranging from literature to horror films, and creating, unwittingly, the modern horror genre. Some musicians drew on this poetic depth of uncertainty to enrich their art. The monsters we hide within ourselves are often more horrible than those of the classic fantastic bestiary, and, in the end, they are only avatars of our deepest – and only too real – troubles. Poe did not have a reputation as a great optimist. Flirting with madness, overwhelmed by anguish and depression, his feelings all appear at the heart of his stories, and he is far from the only fantastic author of whom this is true. The musical genres that most often quote Poe include rock and metal. Aside from the number of groups that have adapted his poems (**Arcturus**, **Sopor Aeternus**) or have paid homage to him (**Iron Maiden**, **The Alan Parsons Project**, and **Nightwish** with their striking pendulum on *Dark Passion Play*), a natural connection is made with metal when we know that the themes of time passing, loneliness, depression and madness are very common in that musical genre. The cover of *Angst* by **Todtgelichter** expresses this in poetic and dizzying fashion, showing a figure sinking into an infinite oceanic emptiness. There is even a subgenre, depressive suicidal black metal, that is totally devoted to the psychological or existential suffering that sometimes drives people to suicide. This is depicted in striking  fashion by the black and white cover of the album *Halmstad* by **Shining**, which features a full-face photograph of a woman with a pistol pointing into her mouth. Sometimes this fantasy-haunted darkness becomes reality: **Per Yngve Ohlin**, better known by his stage name, **Dead**, and the second vocalist of **Mayhem**, is a sadly iconic example of this. He died by suicide, and a photograph of his dead body later served as the cover for a live album by the group. His distinctive use of corpse paint, his voice, which sounded as if it came from beyond the grave, and his troubling behaviour accentuated even more the phantasmagorical, sinister aura of black metal's second wave. His brief time on Earth, and his highly particular story, forged the dark legend of black metal. Before shooting himself, he took the time to write a note, apologizing for any bloodstains on the sofa, thus leaving this world on a fairly brutal note of deadpan humour that was appropriate to a fatalistic spirit.

Todtgelichter – *Angst*
Psychotic Waltz – *A Social Grace*

Vlad III, Voivode of Wallachia, had the annoying habit of torturing his victims by impaling them and putting them on public display; that is how he got his nickname 'Vlad Tepes' (the Impaler). However, another of his nicknames was none other than 'Draculea' (Son of the Dragon), and it is from him that Bram Stoker drew inspiration for the name of his fictional count, thus bringing into being the modern myth of the vampire: Dracula. The symbolism and conventions attached to the vampire fit perfectly with the prerequisites of the metal aesthetic. With a black cape, sharp teeth and a cadaverous complexion, the vampire goes out only at night, and has a horror of crucifixes. The vampire is immortal, sexual, seductive, manipulative and charismatic. He is the perfect gothic-romantic icon, as the album covers of **Type O Negative**, **Cradle of Filth**, and **Tribulation** demonstrate. Noble and distinguished, a recluse in his castle, he appeals to cursed artists and those who want to escape society. Also worth mentioning is Anne Rice's *The Vampire Chronicles*, the characters and themes of which would become influential, especially the adventures of Lestat. The Italian group **Theatres des Vampires** drew their name directly from these novels. Despite a few rare examples, such as the krautrock group **Nosferatu**, formed in 1968, the rock of the 1960s and 1970s was not overly full of references to the vampire myth. In 1978, **Shakin' Street** released the album *Vampire Rock*, and **Blue Öyster Cult** released the song 'Nosferatu' in 1979; but these seem more like anecdotal nods than real works exploring a concept. It was with the emergence of gothic rock at the end of the 1970s that the vampire myth began to occupy a more structural place within music. In 1979, **Bauhaus** released the song 'Bela Lugosi's Dead' – a direct reference to the actor who had played Count Dracula in the film directed by Tod Browning, and to the play *Dracula*, based on the novel. Another homage to Bela Lugosi was a series of guitars made by ESP, designed in collaboration with **Kirk Hammett**, a member of **Metallica**. 'Bela Lugosi's Dead' describes black capes, bats flying out of a bell tower, and young virgins crossing a cemetery. A multitude of groups took up this iconography in a direct reference to the gothic novel and, more specifically, to the vampire myth. **Bauhaus** are considered one of the central pillars of gothic rock, and their aesthetic was echoed by artists

such as **Christian Death** and **Fields of the Nephilim**. It should be noted that during this period, gothic rock eschewed the excessively theatrical aspect of glam rock in favour of a more sober, nihilistic attitude. The uninhibited, sequined aspect returned a little later with some bands, such as the Finnish group **The 69 Eyes**, who incidentally wanted to be known as the Helsinki Vampires. In a less glamorous idiom, it was, above all, black metal that embraced the vampire, with groups such as **Vlad Tepes**, **Ancient** and **Mütiilation**, who set aside the dandy aspect to come back to the historical side of the myth's origin, with some even going so far as to make quite pointed references, such as **Basarab**, whose name is the family name of Vlad III.

THE BEST OF *Helsinki Vampires*

The 69 Eyes – *The Best of Helsinki Vampires*
Vlad Tepes – *An Ode to Our Ruin*
Basarab – *Pride of Older Times*

THE SHADOW OF H. P. LOVECRAFT

Lovecraft built a veritable literary empire in the shadows. Gripped by a kind of darkness that was all his own, tinged with frustration and madness, he was able to put into words the existential anguish of an age, to the point of influencing the whole of the 20th-century horror genre. Rooted in the indescribable terror that crouches in the labyrinth of time and perception, Lovecraft's work is as dark as it is unique. It is therefore especially difficult to convey the breadth and wretchedness of the concepts portrayed in his writings. It is difficult, too, to describe faithfully the situations and torments into which he plunges his protagonists. Yet countless film-makers, artists, writers, game designers and indeed musicians have ventured to do so. From 1965 onwards, there is concrete evidence of the influence he exerted on musicians, for that was the year the rock label Dunwich Records was founded – its name a homage to Lovecraft's 1929 novella *The Dunwich Horror*. The label's catalogue even included a compilation featuring the psychedelic rock group that went by the name **H. P. Lovecraft**. On their first album, **Black Sabbath** titled one of their tracks 'Beyond the Wall of Sleep', a reference to Lovecraft's short story of the same name; while **Caravan**, on their album *For Girls Who Grow Plump in the Night*, included a song called 'C'thlu Thlu'. Bands who have paid homage to the writer from Providence include **Iron Maiden**, **Metallica**, **Mercyful Fate** and more too numerous to list here. Ever since, Lovecraft has been the fantastic author featured most often in extreme music. The death metal of the Australian group **Portal** is considered 'Lovecraftian' – as well as the themes it deals with, the music is as if out of reach, featuring chords and rhythms that are absolutely impenetrable. Their secret was so closely guarded that some adventurous guitarists who succeeded in

deciphering their riffs found themselves obliged to delete, at the group's request, the tablature they had created. From 1992, **Cradle of Filth** plunged listeners into horrific Victorian worlds, and the singer **Dani Filth** admitted that he drew inspiration from Lovecraft's novels when writing his lyrics, to the point that he entitled one of the group's compilation albums *Lovecraft and Witch Hearts*. **The Great Old Ones** incorporated the writer into their line-up outright. He is present everywhere: in the lyrics, in the visuals, and even on stage – his portrait on a backcloth, looking out over the stage with a jaded expression, created a destabilizing atmosphere by its mere presence. **Innsmouth**, **Corpsessed**, **Arkham Witch**, **Nile** and hundreds of others have adopted the abundant heritage left behind by this genius of horror, in order to develop their identity.

Innsmouth – *Consumed by Elder Sign*
Arkham Witch – *Get Thothed Vol. 1*
Puteraeon – *The Empires of Death*

THE GREAT OLD ONES

One of the most notable among the many conceptual strokes of Lovecraft's genius is the creation of an original, legendary cosmogony, which was even endowed with an invented language. The writer created the Great Old Ones – omnipotent cosmic entities. They are indescribable, present since the dawn of time, and indifferent to the fate of humans; the mere sight of them can render someone mad. These concepts remained fairly vague in the author's writings. 'No one could describe the monster; no language could portray this vision of madness, this chaos of inarticulate cries, this hideous contradiction of all the laws of matter and of the cosmic order'. We are indebted to Lovecraft's posthumous editor, his friend the writer August Derleth, for a more substantial definition of the Great Old Ones, as well as the conceptualization of the myth of Cthulhu. And of all the creatures that make up the 'Lovecraftian' bestiary, Cthulhu is without a doubt the most emblematic. It is often referenced, revisited, even hijacked, and is now an integral part of pop culture, especially now that Lovecraft's works are out of copyright. It is a contradictory fate that this extraterrestrial kraken has become an icon, for the unspeakable abomination it is supposed to represent should never have earned so much popular success. Furthermore, Lovecraft's descriptions are sufficiently indefinite that they set our imaginations to work. But Cthulhu has become a cult and, as such, it needs to be accompanied by a powerful iconography. The representation of an idol must be instantly identifiable. This Great Old One is thus often depicted as a humanoid with the head of an octopus and the build of a giant. It is characterized by its colossal size and its tentacled, antediluvian appearance. All these artworks – nightmarish, dripping with pseudopodiums and repulsive stringiness – spring from such descriptions. It is the shapeless man-octopus, the guardian of the gateway to outer space. It is the chaotic, absurd entanglement that invades space and time. Cthulhu, in essence, is this indescribable monster, so immense that it connects the bottom of the oceans to the cosmos, while ripping apart the space-time continuum. It has contempt for the human race, regarding it as an insignificant quantity – which chimes perfectly with the cosmic and misanthropic outlook of some groups. 'In its abode of R'lyeh, the deceased Cthulhu awaits, dreaming.'

The Great Old Ones – *EOD: A Tale of Dark Legacy*

Cruciamentum – *Convocation of Crawling Chaos*

Sulphur Aeon – *Gateway to the Antisphere*

Sulphur Aeon – *Swallowed by the Ocean's Tide*

Of all musical genres, metal features the most mascots. The first example that springs to mind is, of course, Eddie the Head, the totem figure of **Iron Maiden**: a 'zombiesque' entity with sharp fangs, screaming death. With each new album release, Eddie is depicted in different situations and distinct historical periods. He is seen as a pharaoh in ancient Egypt, as a fighter pilot during the Second World War, in a cyberpunk dystopia, in Hell, in a padded cell… Eddie literally embodies **Iron Maiden**, to the point that this character, invented by the artist Derek Riggs, is almost more famous than the group. He even appears in the shape of a gigantic, animated puppet at their concerts. A mascot provides a common thread between albums, and allows a group to create a cult around an anti-heroic figure akin to the monsters of the movies. And the connection is no coincidence, for the mascot is descended from the culture of horror films, where the evil entity is often more striking than the protagonists. Since metal takes pride in aiming to induce a form of deviance mixed with fascination, it is after all a fairly logical connection. In the same tradition as posters for slasher films, an album cover is seen as a visual punch in the guts – an image that throws you off balance but that, insidiously, makes you want to discover what is behind it. Although Eddie often eclipses his counterparts on other covers, we should not forget Snaggletooth, the demonic bull that adorns the albums of **Motörhead**, or Vic Rattlehead, the humanoid with a skull in place of a head, created for the group **Megadeth**. In the same spirit, other groups, such as **Lich King**, **Skeletonwitch** and **Iced Earth**, have also opted for a demon with a skull for a head. The choice of mascot says a lot about a group's musical aims and aesthetic: **Sodom** chose a brute – half soldier, half executioner – **HammerFall** a Viking, while **Running Wild** opted for Adrian, a pirate and werewolf… The recurrent depiction of such emblematic creatures creates a sense of coherence, and shapes the mythology of the group's

world. Most mascots aim to be menacing and powerful, and their appearance is often so totally exaggerated that it verges on bad taste. Among the most original and worthy of mention are the mascot of **Quiet Riot**, a man with an iron mask who has escaped from a psychiatric hospital, and that of **Dangerous Toys**, a huge, wicked clown: a sort of cross between Pennywise from Stephen King's *It* and the creatures in Stephen Chiodo's *Killer Klowns from Outer Space*.

Motörhead – *Overkill*
Iron Maiden – *Powerslave*
Motörhead – *Orgasmatron*

MYTHI HEROIS

MYTHS OF THE HERO

In the psychedelic hallucinations depicted on trippy rock album covers, it was already sometimes possible to glimpse a magical creature, a mystical figure or an enchanting landscape. Some album covers were real, little windows opening on to enchanted worlds in which artists, designers and musicians tried to ensnare the listener. Progressive rock then continued this trend into the 1980s. Its long, varied instrumental tracks opened up more space for new concepts, and the supernatural found a very special place there. The painter Roger Dean left his mark on many album covers, and contributed enormously to the spread of an epic aura that pervades a large number of creations from the period. Today, all branches of metal have incorporated elements of fantasy into their frames of reference. Heavy metal, melodic speed metal and symphonic power metal groups tend towards the grandiose, otherworldly aspect of high fantasy, while more extreme genres, such as black metal and death metal, connect more directly to the vehicle of myths and legends, taking an approach that is often more solemn and dark. What all these groups have in common, however, is that they are more melodic than average, giving prominence to vigorous, bold, epic riffs. Today, almost all the great high-fantasy authors are represented. There are even some groups that formed with the sole purpose of paying homage to a saga: **Narnia** for *The Chronicles of Narnia*, **Skroth** for *Game of Thrones*, **Myrddraal** for *The Wheel of Time*, and **Caladan Brood** for *Malazan Book of the Fallen*. Some have even gone so far as to create a whole lore to go with their music. By carefully reading the lyrics of an album, it is possible to follow the fates of the heroes and peoples with which these imaginary worlds are teeming. **Gloryhammer**, in a very light fantasy idiom, tell the story of Angus McFife's fight against the abominable Zargothrax, while **Rhapsody of Fire**, in their first five albums, sing the Emerald

Sword Saga and subsequently continue to develop other stories. The principle of building a saga around albums occurs above all in symphonic and progressive metal – genres that often come close to opera and so are perfectly suited to narrative. The musicians share with gamemasters the power to carry us to a world full of marvels and darkness, firing the imagination of the listener, and even reawakening the child that sleeps within every one of us.

Yes – *Relayer*
Skroth – *Skys Over Westeros*

RINGS

In their song 'Ramble On', **Led Zeppelin** invoke Mordor and Gollum to symbolize the torment enveloping the song's narrator. 'The Wizard' by **Black Sabbath** was inspired by the character of Gandalf, and the magician's trail can be traced right back to 1965 when **Gandalf**, the psychedelic rock group whose name explicitly pays homage to the grey pilgrim, were formed. In December 1970, the Silence label released an album with the sober title *Music Inspired by Lord of the Rings*. It is the work of **Bo Hansson**, a Swedish rock musician in tune with the spirit of the times, who was gripped by a creative surge after burying himself in Tolkien's books. Proof that from the infancy of hard rock and metal, the author had already captured the imagination of many musicians. Along with H. P. Lovecraft, who did not live as long, Tolkien is one of the architects of modern mythology, and his work has influenced the way in which a saga is narrated. He brought to life a world that is astonishing in its depth: Tolkien imagined a story spanning millennia, and invented languages, entire kingdoms, family trees and more. It is in part thanks to his works that people first conceived of the expanded universe. His stories are so detailed and so full of symbols that they changed the way people thought about fantasy – including the musicians that drew inspiration from them. However, if there is a single group that has been able to plunge its listeners, body and soul, into the world of Middle-earth, a group that has captured all the evocative power of this legendary saga, it is **Summoning**. The visuals of their albums say a great deal about the group's ability to enable us to live the Tolkien experience through a profound, atmospheric black metal tinged with orchestral influences and role-playing game music. Tolkien is also one of the foundations of the heavy metal played by the German group **Blind Guardian**. Today,

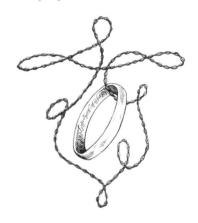

the group are regarded by audiences as one of the greatest power metal bands, and thousands of fans at their concerts join in singing songs such as 'Lord of the Rings' and 'The Bard's Song' in chorus. Shrouded in darkness and much more conversant with Mordor, the black metal scene is bursting with references to Sauron, his henchmen and the various foul places over which he rules. The infernal region of Middle-earth and the nefarious atmosphere that reigns there are a source of almost endless inspiration that enriches the worlds of these groups. **Gorgoroth**, **Balrog**, **Cirith Gorgor** and **Lugburz** are all names that feature on black metal album covers and refer directly to places and creatures that are straight out of the imagination of the English linguist.

Blind Guardian – *Tales From the Twilight World*
Cirith Gorgor – *Unveiling the Essence*
Bo Hansson – *Music Inspired by Lord of the Rings*

Robert E. Howard also created a legend: that of Conan the Barbarian. Even before this character burst on to the big screen in the extremely muscular shape of Arnold Schwarzenegger, Conan had revolutionized heroic fantasy in the pages of the magazine *Weird Tales*. The adventures of the Cimmerian barbarian, and their violent, epic and sometimes disillusioned nature, mixing the elements of a tribal and magical historical timeline, made a lasting impression. But it was not until a supremely gifted painter and illustrator came on board that Conan entered the pantheon of the collective imagination. It was indeed thanks to the vision of Frank Frazetta that Conan came to life and his image was modernized. With role-playing games seeing an explosion in popularity at the time, the artist left a permanent mark on the generations that encountered him, and during the 1970s album covers quietly appeared that were clearly inspired by Frazetta – such as *Hard Attack* by **Dust** – and some even featured scenes directly borrowed from his work. But the musical style that plunged head-first into sword and sorcery was the true heavy metal of the 1980s – with **Manowar** clearly spearheading this movement. It was very rare at this time to find a group that did not make allusions to the literature, movies and role-playing games of their childhood. The 1980s were, incidentally, also the time when dark fantasy was beginning to appear on the big screen. With regards to groups, it was a crowded field, with **Manilla Road**, **Virgin Steele** and **Omen** in America, and **Heavy Load**, **Sortilège** and **Attack** in Europe. Riffs were sometimes heavy and aggressive, and at other times rapid and heroic. As for the songs' lyrics, they were permeated with this dark, violent and often melancholy fantasy. Heroic fantasy can also be found in the music of groups inspired by the novels of Michael Moorcock, and especially his saga of the Eternal Champion. The English novelist pushed the genre into ever more astonishing and strange corners, sometimes to the limit of psychedelia. It is no surprise that **Hawkwind** and **Moorcock** collaborated on several albums, notably *Warrior on the Edge of Time* and *The Chronicle of the Black Sword*.

Moorcock's principal hero, Elric of Melniboné, is not the archetypal hero: rather than being a big, burly man full of testosterone, he is a slender albino with a pale complexion and ruby-coloured eyes. He confronts the philosophical concepts of order and chaos, communicates directly with the gods, explores dreams and parallel dimensions, and more. The alluring magic these stories emanate casts its spell on a huge number of other groups, including **Cirith Ungol** (Elric features on all their covers), **Skelator**, **Dark Moor**, **Eternal Champion** and **Blind Guardian**.

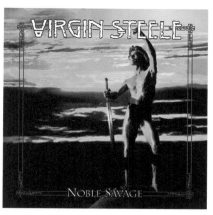

Manilla Road – *Crystal Logic*
Virgin Steele – *Noble Savage*
Dust – *Hard Attack*

The term 'heavy metal' was first used in music during the 1960s, referring to a kind of rock that was heavier rhythmically, and massive as steel. Ever since its emergence, heavy metal made full use of this label to form its identity. The words 'iron', 'steel' and 'metal' were used at every opportunity for the names of record labels, groups, albums, songs and festivals. Some even based their entire imagery on this vocabulary: **Anvil**, **Sacred Steel**, **Medieval Steel**, **Ironsword**. For in metal, steel above all denotes bladed weapons, flails, axes and swords. As we have seen, heavy metal and power metal are steeped in the warlike images of heroic fantasy, and consequently in those genres there are blades absolutely everywhere. They pierce through logos or lend more power to lettering. Sometimes they can even be used as the sole subject for the design of a cover, but, more often than not, they are raised against the enemy, in the hands of a tough guy ready to do battle. The singer of **Eternal Champion**, a blacksmith by trade, sometimes goes on stage carrying a sword he made himself. From the cover artwork for *Wargods of Metal* by **Sacred Steel** to that of *The Armor of Ire* by **Eternal Champion**, the conquering aesthetic of a warrior who has raised his sword to the sky in victory or as a call to arms is glorified. This whole imaginary world of battle, which, since Frazetta, has taken on a fairly phallic, virile aspect, implicitly harks back to the noblest values established by Arthurian legend, and especially the most famous sword in literature: Excalibur. Often confused with the Sword in the Stone, in the popular imagination it is associated with the blade of the chosen one – the knight selected by destiny – which, like the music that references it, gives the impression of the invincibility of the person who brandishes it. Inspired as much by the first promotional photographs for **Venom** as by dark fantasy, the second generation of black metal created a standardized neo-medieval imagery of war sometimes verging on kitsch, in a style that was more trivial and determinedly morbid. Worth mentioning among the most emblematic images of this trend is the photograph of the young **Varg Vikernes**, posing with a mass of weapons for his **Burzum** project; the cover of *Sons of Northern Darkness* by **Immortal**, which shows the musicians wearing armour and in a combat pose; and images of the members of **Satyricon** on a throne or in the snow, holding in their hands everything they need to slay all their detractors. Not to mention the metal spikes and other rusty nails, sometimes disproportionately big, that adorn the stage outfits of certain musicians: every little helps to draw us into a dark, medieval dream world.

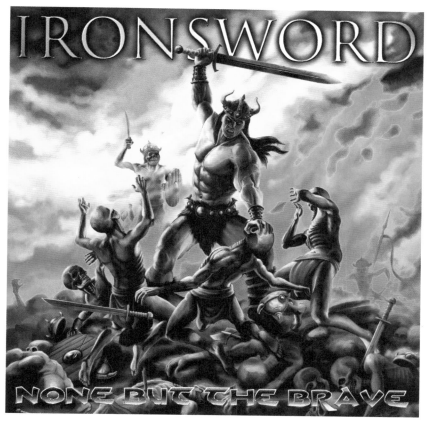

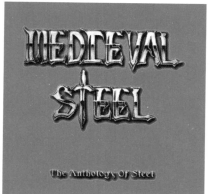

Eternal Champion – *The Armor of Ire*
Medieval Steel – *The Anthology of Steel*
Ironsword – *None but the Brave*
Sacred Steel – *Wargods of Metal*
Maniac Butcher – *Krvestřeb*

Although the 'dragonish' creatures of Roger Dean, which feature on the iconic covers of **Asia**, for example, come from Asian myths, it is dragons of Western origin that are most often encountered in the rock and metal bestiary. The Asian dragon is longer, more slender, and does not always have wings. It is linked to the forces of nature but is not synonymous with hostility. It can be seen in the work of groups that espouse Asian culture, such as the live album *Rising* by **Dream Spirit**. The European dragon, on the other hand, resembles a large, winged, agile serpent. Popular culture has made it into a supreme beast: the boss at the end of the dungeon in role-playing games, the ancestral guardian of a hidden treasure in literature, and the star of special effects in movies and TV shows. The dragon spits purifying fire, can fly, and has gigantic claws and sharp fangs; its blood even has magical properties. Furthermore, the dragon is usually endowed with great intelligence. It is a devastating autonomous weapon that is almost always unstoppable. That is, incidentally, the reason why, in heavy metal and power metal, there is usually a tendency to want to slay the dragon – just as **Dio** have done on stage. The forces of good have to prevail over the vile one – this is how the most conventional heroic fantasy tales unfold – although sometimes the dragon helps the hero, as in *Tales of Ancient Prophecies* by **Twilight Force**. The dragon is unquestionably the most iconic magical creature in metal. If it also embodies chaos and darkness, it is because Christianity has made it the symbol of the Apocalypse, the representation of the Beast in its most ferocious, pagan form. In the New Testament, the serpent symbolizes evil and is described as a great dragon, an ancient serpent called 'devil'. And what is the Leviathan, which appears in the Bible, if not a giant marine dragon? It is not the commonest of anti-Christian symbols, but it is this folkloric version of the dragon that features a great deal in death metal and black metal. **Leviathan** is also the name of a cult American depressive suicidal black metal group. When someone chooses to side with the dragon, they have taken the side of evil and domination, with the risk that a knight in shining armour will exact retribution.

Twilight Force – *Tales of Ancient Prophecies*
Dream Spirit – *Rising*
Asia – *Asia*

Merlin, a figure from the myth of the Knights of the Round Table who has been labelled a wizard ever since his appearance in the Walt Disney movie *The Sword in the Stone*, has become the archetype of the sorcerer or magician. He is a legendary figure with near-divine powers, who has witnessed the passage of the centuries. With cultural roots that predate Christianity, the myths he conjures up are an extraordinary source of inspiration, as much for literature, cinema and games as for music. When fantasy became a little more widespread in the world of music, thanks to the progressive rock of the 1970s, magicians came forth from their lairs and swarmed over the landscape. The magician brought with him all his mystique, appearing as an absolute form of wisdom and erudition that was the perfect accompaniment to an increasingly complex kind of rock that aligned itself with the supernatural. When they did not deal with medieval themes, songs always evoked escapism and dreams.

Magicians are often the earliest witnesses to imaginary worlds, sometimes adopting the role of a bard who relates the mystical visions of a forgotten past. The French progressive rock group **Atoll** went so far as to name an album *Musiciens magiciens* (Magician Musicians), while for **Uriah Heep**, a magician armed with a wand introduces himself as our guide on the cover of *Demons and Wizards*. Not so surprisingly, heavy metal and power metal also feature old, bearded, all-powerful wizards, in the cause of a sugar-coated fantasy tinged with kitsch and a certain naivety. But where magicians have found a place most often is in stoner doom, a subgenre in which the words 'witch' and 'wizard' pop up everywhere. Only a clairvoyant being, endowed with supernatural powers, can guide the listener through the thick fog of mystery and the occult that emanates from this genre of music. Like a preparer of potions bent over his cauldron, the musician concocts his own sound identity so as to find the perfect alchemy with the power to carry the listener into a whirlwind of hallucinatory riffs. In symphonic black metal especially, the magician adopts a much darker and more malevolent position, for he is draped in a cape, and you hardly ever see his face. He hides from the rest of the world and plots silently against humans, for whom he has only modest compassion. He is turned towards the heavens, communicates with the stars, and seems to invoke mysterious, evil forces. Such is his power that sometimes he even manages to become one with the cosmos, for his omniscience allows him to play with the elements and the planets. In the lyrics to 'I Am the Black Wizards' by **Emperor**, a supreme wizard spews out his evil omnipotence, while on the cover of *Reign in Supreme Darkness* by **Vargrav**, he defends his realm from the tops of black, misty mountains.

Vargrav – *Reign in Supreme Darkness*
Merlin – *The Wizard*
Limbonic Art – *In Abhorrence Dementia*
Uriah Heep – *Demons and Wizards*
Gryphon – *Red Queen to Gryphon Three*

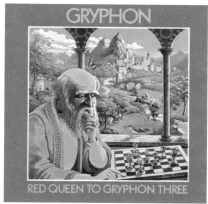

TROLLS

A supernatural creature, secluded in the mountains or the forests, the troll is perhaps the most recurrent magical figure in metal after the dragon. It is a figure from Nordic mythology, and the embodiment of the magic forces of nature. Rather hostile to humans, sometimes malevolent and violent, it takes on a different appearance, size and shape depending on the legend in question. Although it is less emblematic than other mythical creatures, it has stood the test of time – its reign has lasted from the origins of Nordic mythology to the present day. With the arrival of modern fantasy during the 20th century, the troll enjoyed a resurgence in interest, from the work of Tolkien to tabletop and card games such as *Dungeons & Dragons* and *Magic: The Gathering*. The predominance of fantasy and Nordic myths in the metal genre explains why the troll appears on certain albums. Its unfriendly, even dangerous image makes it a familiar choice for a good number of black metal groups: trolls lurk in their lyrics, their artworks, or simply in the names they have chosen for themselves. At least 15 groups have the word 'troll' in their name, always with the aim of tending towards the dark side of Nordic folk myth. The troll may therefore herald music that is violent and makes no concessions, that is evil and impossible to tame, and that reeks of pillage and atrocities, as in the case of the group **Troll**. But in the collective imagination, as if stuck with the body shape of an ape-like, slightly awkward giant, the troll has come to exude a friendliness all on its own. Indeed, during the 20th century, its portrayals grew increasingly inoffensive and childlike, to the point that the creature completely ceased to be frightening. The troll became a clumsy, even slightly stupid humanoid. This is often the way trolls are depicted in animated films and strip cartoons, and if there is a subgenre in which this archetype of the troll is present, it is folk metal.

Trollfest readily enliven their bouncy metal music with a bouzouki, saxophone or accordion, all the better to adhere to the festive, explosive character of the trolls that they portray. The pioneers and biggest exponents of the genre are the Finnish group **Finntroll**, who position themselves somewhere between the traditional view of trolls and the most sugar-coated representations. This comes through in their music, which is sometimes dark and savage, at other times direct and dance-like, but always tinged with enchantment. Some groups have toyed with the idea of troll metal in the same way as people speak of goblin metal, with reference to groups that have fun with that other mythical creature.

Litvintroll – *Rock'n'Troll*
Troll – *Drep de Kristne*

In order to parody or distort a culture in a meaningful way, it is necessary to know it, to have been sufficiently immersed in it – even to have been part of it – so as to have the required perspective on what drives it and makes it so distinct and typical. That is how Terry Pratchett managed to attain a place of honour in fantasy literature with his *Discworld* series. He achieved this while cleverly twisting clichés and interpreting the codes of fantasy in a humorous way, but always and above all with passion. A similar approach is taken by groups such as **Nanowar**, who made it their mission to parody – affectionately – the group **Manowar** and the clichés linked to fantasy in the metal scene. Following legal problems, the cult group **Rhapsody** were obliged to change their name to **Rhapsody of Fire**, so **Nanowar** also changed their name to **Nanowar of Steel**. This love of cliché and quotation can be felt even in the songs of groups that aim to compose easy melodies that can be sung in chorus rather than to write revolutionary material. The chord sequences are often predictable, and that is what renders them agreeable and accessible to all. Stereotypes and codes manage to be so clunky in metal that it is sometimes hard to distinguish between what is serious and what is parody. While many groups drift into paying homage clumsily but

sincerely, others, such as **Gloryhammer** and **Helloween**, do not hesitate to add a healthy dose of humour while at the same time making sure they create a world that is rich enough, and albums that are accomplished enough, that the listener feels a real desire to plunge into the adventure they narrate. Even though the music may be metallic and rapid, it is always tinged with a certain positivity, and epic, rousing anthems are preferred to morbid or dissonant laments. The link with role-playing is seen in their desire to tell stories and have fun. It should be noted that **Naheulband** (the musical version of the famous humorous audio sagas of *Le Donjon de Naheulbeuk* (The Dungeon of Naheulbeuk), created by **John Lang**) sometimes take part in metal festivals, and that some of their compositions are obvious nods to groups such as **Finntroll** and **Rhapsody of Fire**. Indeed, their guitarist is **Tony Beaufils**, who is also the guitarist of the symphonic power metal group **Qantice**. All of this suggests a certain amount of self-mockery, which never fails to come as a surprise in a field of music that can, on the surface at least, seem so abstruse and grotesque.

Helloween – *Keeper of the Seven Keys: Part II*
Nanowar of Steel – *A Knight at the Opera*

MYSTERIA COSMI

THE MYSTERIES
OF THE COSMOS

In 1977, the sleeve of the very cultish *News of the World* by **Queen** was inspired by Isaac Asimov's *I, Robot* at the request of the drummer, **Roger Taylor**, a science fiction fan. Looking back through the history of rock and roll, we can see that **Jimi Hendrix** was keen on science fiction literature and that certain songs by **Frank Zappa** are inhabited by strange creatures and characters worthy of veritable science fiction stories. However, it was with the heavy metal of the 1980s that cyborgs, killer artificial intelligence, and other android creatures invaded the landscape of rock music. **Judas Priest** made such entities iconic, with a mechanised figure riding a motorbike on *Painkiller*, and another transformed into a fiery machine on *Firepower*. The group even pushed the design of robots into even more unexpected territory, with the gleaming animal machines that appear on *Defenders of the Faith* and *Screaming for Vengeance*. Elsewhere, we can find warrior robots, as in the case of **Liege Lord** with their album *Master Control*, and **Voivod**, who built part of their identity around Korgull, a devastating cyborg soldier. The 1980s saw the birth in cinema of mythical machines such as Terminator, Robocop, the Decepticons of the *Transformers* series, and many other vengeful robots. The iconic cover of *Hypertrace* by **Scanner** pays vibrant homage to these movies, which were to encounter worldwide success and greatly inspire the worlds of film, literature and video games, but also the world of music. The more time that passed, the harder metal became, and the more sophisticated and disturbing these iron machines became. They were so dominant that sometimes they fused with living beings and ended up enslaving humankind. Industrial metal and cyber metal questioned transhumanism and the relationship between human and machine even more directly, as in the artwork on *SETI* by **The Kovenant**, a group that, on stage, went so far as to make themselves up to look like androids, in a style reminiscent of the aesthetic of the manga *Blame!*, an icon of cyberpunk culture. In these subgenres,

album covers reflected musical content with profound accuracy. This music often seems dehumanized – very cleanly produced, clinical, featuring electronic sounds obtained from samples, and drum machines that emit a robotic riff. These groups succeed in conveying perfectly the horror and fascination evoked by the idea of transhumanism and robotization pushed to their extremes, within a space where distinction can no longer be made between human and machine. The end result, unsurprisingly, is quite far removed from any kind of utopia, as the artworks of **Sybreed** suggest so well. If we play God too much, we risk our creation one day turning against us.

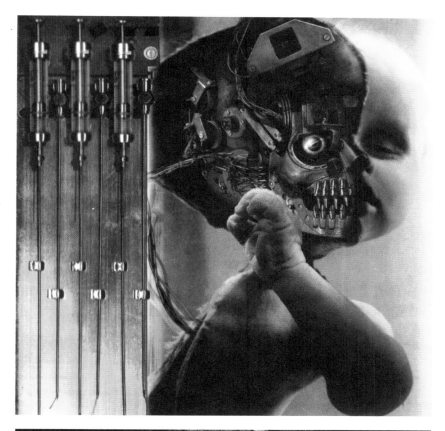

The Kovenant – *SETI*
Sybreed – *God is an Automaton*
Sybreed – *Slave Design*

SPACESHIPS

During the 1960s, at the height of the Cold War and with the Space Race in full swing, the hippie movement blossomed, along with the whole drug culture attached to it. It became normal for many artists and music lovers to leave behind dreary reality and raise their minds to wider, brighter horizons. All those fantasies around the conquest of space, with the promise it held of discovering unexplored worlds, provided a veritable crucible of inspiration for the artists of the time. Some even used the term 'space rock' for groups such as **Hawkwind** and **Amon Düül**, whose sounds sometimes even suggested extraterrestrial music or seemed to have been created at the instrument panel of a spacecraft's cockpit. Humans walked on the moon for the first time on 21 July 1969, at a time when first progressive rock and then hard rock were making their appearance. The cosmos became a new sphere for artistic, sound and visual experimentation. Some album covers truly bore witness to the retrofuturism that was in vogue at the time – featuring starry skies, spacecraft with improbable shapes, and multicoloured planets. Heavy metal, and subsequently thrash metal, borrowed freely from the world of science fiction. Drawing on influences such as

Star Wars, *Star Trek*, *Alien* and magazines such as *Métal Hurlant* (Screaming Metal), some of these groups explored the themes of the space-time continuum and intergalactic travel. Indeed, it is a genre bursting with concept albums. Today, it is not rare to come across metal groups with progressive overtones that also immerse themselves in science fiction, playing music that is rich in imagery and narrative, describing action that took place a long time ago, in a distant galaxy. In a much more dystopian idiom, grind metal and death metal groups that tackle this theme show us a more sinister facet of the future. In these portrayals, alien entities enslave populations in secret Martian laboratories where humanoid bodies are heaped into ovens, and whole cities are ravaged by lethal viruses… When it comes to dressing up vigorous, complex, brutal music that explores the most fascinating branches of the tree of possibilities, illustrators have not been short of imagination. This often takes the form of an explosion of colours, with impressive attention to detail, as can be seen in the work of the unmissable **Pär Olofsson**.

Q5 – *Steel the Light*
Hawkwind – *Hall of the Mountain Grill*

In 1979, the phrase on the poster for the movie *Alien* announced that 'in space, no one can hear you scream' – but it seems that, since then, some groups have tried to take up the challenge. Metal and cosmicism go well together, especially atmospheric black metal, of which **Darkspace** have become the spearhead, with their extremely dark album covers that aim to suck the listener's soul into fascinating, hypnotic black holes. There is a kind of gloomy profundity, an inexpressible vertigo, in the contemplation of infinite, cruel space where we are not welcome. On the album cover of *Muukalainen puhuu* (The Stranger Speaks), the group **Oranssi Pazuzu** show us an astronaut who is lost in a dark vision of space where the traveller is no longer any more than a shadow of himself. While the Hubble Space Telescope has flooded us with highly appealing colourized photographs of the galaxies that surround us, space is the hostile environment par excellence, and it embodies, by its very nature, the unknown. In the understanding of it lie the secrets of the world and the origins of life, but still we struggle to penetrate them. Here, we are quite close to a kind of terror on which Lovecraft drew abundantly. The artwork on *Pupil of the Searing Maelstrom* by the Icelandic group **Almyrkvi** depicts a colourless galaxy that takes the form of a cosmic eye, which gazes at us from within dark matter. In a more naive but equally explicit manner, the cover of **Midnight Odyssey**'s *Funerals from the Astral Sphere* features an illustration of death praying to a comet that glows red in the Milky Way. The goal of this kind of visual is to make us feel minuscule in the face of the terrifying forces of the cosmos. Taking on an element of science fiction, the enigmatic cover of *Spheres*, by the group **Pestilence**, depicts a sharp-pointed, menacing spherical structure (the group's mascot, in a way) hurtling at full speed towards a black hole that awaits it at the

galaxy's heart. It is a reminder that, from *Doom* to *Event Horizon* and *Dead Space*, movies and video games have been able to capitalize on this demonic presence in the darkest depths of space. It is as if our Earth is a bubble of oxygen and relative peace in the heart of a cosmic primeval soup that will eventually engulf us. With the visual on their album *Horizonless*, **Loss** produced the most romantic vision of the genre. A sort of gigantic, scrawny creature, the size of a colossus, tugs on part of the Milky Way as if pulling on a sheet, in the process revealing the infinite, dark abyss that is hidden by the falsely enchanting blanket of the stars.

Darkspace – *Darkspace I*
Almyrkvi – *Pupil of the Searing Maelstrom*

FRACTALS

Thanks to the arrival of software such as Photoshop, the 2000s saw the blossoming of artworks with a highly pronounced digital aesthetic. While some saw this as a sign of poor mastery of modern tools, others took advantage of the new software to reinforce their music's contemporary, synthetic identity, a little like the movie *Tron* was able to do in its own time. Certain groups, such as **SUP** on their EP *Transfer*, slid into an excess of archaic 3D motifs and saturated colours, whereas others sought simply to destabilize the senses by placing the viewer at the heart of shapeless matrices that were close to optical illusion and kinetic art. This is what **Ulver** did on *Drone Activity* and, in a more mathematical style, what **Cartoon Theory** did on the album *Sacred Geometry*. Several groups pushed the fantasy of the digital further, transforming printed circuit boards or computer programmes into citadels of jade or Escher-like structures. This is what the group **0110111101110110011011 1001101001** succeeded in doing brilliantly on the cover of their album *S/2004 S3*. Groups such as **DragonForce** went deeper into this aesthetic than the artwork on album covers *Matrix* and *Le Cobaye* (The Guinea Pig), as seen more specifically on their cover of *Maximum Overload*, which features a new virtual, cyberpunk universe into which we can immerse ourselves. Still closer towards the infinite, the abstract and the cryptic lie fractals. Our gaze gets lost amid these structures that repeat themselves endlessly, which draw us towards the infinitely large, towards the near-divine, as shown on the cover of *Nothing* by the group **Meshuggah**. We can no longer tell whether the dimensions are immense or infinitely small. We can almost see these visuals, with their symmetrical, repetitive geometry, as a modern response to the psychedelic frenzy of the rock of the 1960s. It is as if these fractals – produced this time by computers – remind us that technology is now capable of creating things that we once regarded as being peculiar to nature. Of course, these groups use new technologies to produce their music and seek to be at the cutting edge. Djent was one of the first musical styles to owe its success to the internet and its new modes of communication – of which the cover of *The Discovery* by **Born of Osiris** is a fine example. This is one of the most modern branches of metal, and surely the genre that uses the most cutting-edge equipment for guitar recording and amplification. This style is technically very exact, and draws its influences as much from jazz as from technical death metal and metalcore. Many purists persist in putting about a 'clichéd' image of the artists in the djent scene as being nerds who are addicted to online guitar tutorials, more preoccupied by the precision of their sound than by pure composition. The genre's main influence, for that matter, is **Meshuggah**, a pioneering Swedish group that based some of their ideas precisely on the coming of a machine-god and the mathematical terror that computers imply.

Ulver – *Drone Activity*
0110111101110110011011001101001 – *S/2004 S3*
SUP – *Transfer*
Meshuggah – *Nothing*

VESTIGIA HISTORIAE

THE REMAINS
OF HISTORY

Of all musical styles, metal is unquestionably the most conceptual. It is such extreme music that it constitutes in itself a markedly artistic approach. It is music into which you have to know how to immerse yourself. So it is no coincidence that the logos of black metal groups are illegible to the newcomer… This is a language for the initiated. An album must work on several levels: music, first of all, for it expresses the most emotion; but after that comes the conceptual framework that will lead whoever listens to this music into a world of mental images. And it is hardly surprising that metal is the genre that features the largest number of concept albums. Many groups create their own mythology, drawn from their own imaginations. However, others embrace an existing mythology that is by nature more realistic: history. And by using it as the foundation upon which to build an artistic universe, a group can give their music a new dimension in the real world and play with our collective memory. When **Departure Chandelier** called their album *Antichrist Rise to Power* and illustrated it with a painting of Napoleon on his deathbed, they created a conversation about the world and our past. Sometimes, albums function as an original soundtrack that illustrates the destiny of a historical figure. With their album *Jehanne*, **Abduction** featured a painting depicting Joan of Arc looking heavenwards, sword in hand: the cover immediately enlightens us as to the concept and invites us to listen to the album, exploring certain key moments in history – episodes that are known to all of us because they are in schoolbooks. The history of this figure, from her origins to her tragic end, conveys a whole mass of sentiments and scenes that take on another dimension when explored through extreme metal. When a historical period provokes a degree of fascination and ideas of darkness, metal can find a way into it,

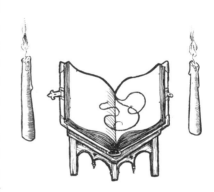

with an approach that can almost come close to that of a musical. Some groups play that card for all it is worth. **Ex Deo**, for example, not content with making an album entitled *Romulus*, which relates the myth of the foundation of Rome, go so far as to play on stage dressed as centurions. In other cases, an image alone has been enough to transport us to a particular period of history. The powerful were guillotined during the French Revolution, and that was excuse enough for the group **Robespierre** to portray the revolutionary in a demonic light, brandishing a severed head while astride a sinister-looking horse. Of course, it is sometimes difficult to make allowances regarding the inevitably political aim behind the invocation of history, a discipline that is plagued by many fantasies and on to which many project a need to regain past greatness. In all cases, combining highly contemporary, violent music with dark moments in history creates a unique dissonance that works astonishingly well and can enliven a period regarded as inherently stale, like everything that belongs to the past.

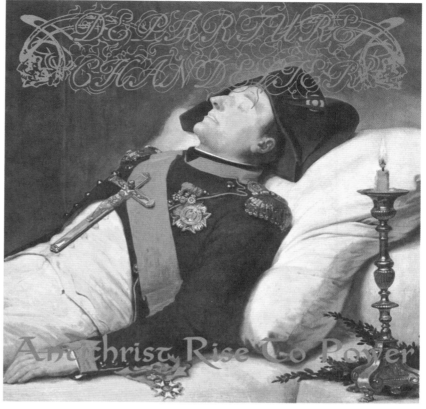

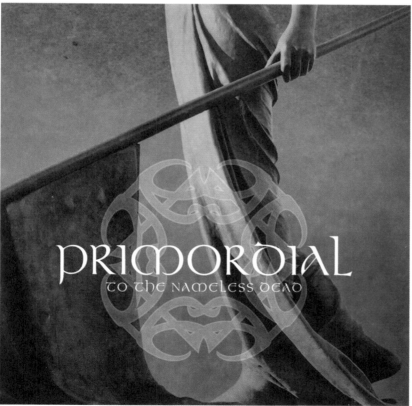

Ex Deo – *Romulus*
Robespierre – *Die You Heathen, Die!*
Departure Chandelier – *Antichrist Rise to Power*
Primordial – *To the Nameless Dead*
Abduction – *Jehanne*

Of the historical periods most visited by metal musicians, the Middle Ages come top of the list. Progressive rock groups had already made use of its aesthetic. The album *The Power and the Glory* by **Gentle Giant** displays a close-up of a playing card that depicts a suspicious-looking king who is drawing a sword from its scabbard. In a more popular and festive vein, the sleeve of *Minstrel in the Gallery* by **Jethro Tull** invites the listener to celebrate with those rock troubadours on their electric choruses. It is clear that even present-day heavy metal has inherited this nostalgia if we look at the cover of the EP *Citadelle* by **Citadelle**, with its Crusader knight contemplating a burning town. It is not surprising to hear military drum rolls as the record opens, along with guitars that play on a loop like heroic trumpets. The names of groups often fit the historical period that they conjure up. This is the case with **Chevalier**, who on their album *Destiny Calls* display a wild romanticism through the image of a knight whose destiny is dark. Chivalry, with the violence, heroism and values that are attached to it, has been fertile ground for many groups who see it as a means to pull in the crowds, brandishing their music like a banner. Black metal is probably the subgenre that has made the most use of it. *Assiégé* (Besieged) by **Véhémence** begins literally with the sound of a sword being drawn from its sheath, as if the album were an echo of the violent din of a battle. The group illustrated their album with a classic painting, to inform us clearly that they intend to take us on a journey through time, fantasizing about the problems within a besieged castle. The message sent out by **Keep of Kalessin** with their album *Armada* is clearer still. Metal is a battle that the musicians wage against their demons and against technical difficulty, and the listener will be a willing victim of this battle. The word 'metal' itself calls to mind the clinking of armour, the clatter of swords striking each other and the sound of shields being crushed under a mass of weapons.

Although this is a period that is doubtless freely embellished, and of which people talk all kinds of nonsense regardless of historical reality, the damage has been done: this historical period acts as a catalyst for all those fantasies of passionate heroism, and sometimes even many archaic and faintly sickening warmongering traditions. Despite everything, the potential of a time of battles and knights to fascinate remains intact, right down to the raw medieval black metal of **Ritual Flail**, who explore the darkness of the vanquished in *He Who Was Lost in Battle*.

Citadelle – *Citadelle*

Gentle Giant – *The Power and the Glory*

Ritual Flail – *He Who Was Lost in Battle*

Chevalier – *Destiny Calls*

CASTLES

At the top of a dark hill silhouetted against a murky sky, there towers an imposing castle. Threatening yet peaceful behind its fortress-like appearance, it holds many fantasies. Ever since the Middle Ages, the castle has been the place where the powerful live. Its lofty position overlooks valleys, and makes it possible to watch out for the enemy. Its size and solidity command respect; it is the refuge of heroes. The fortified castle unquestionably represents power. Conversely, it also functions as a hideout, a final refuge, a form of withdrawal into oneself, which may one day find itself destroyed, so much does it arouse covetousness. On the cover of their album *A Passage to the Towers*, **Darkenhöld** depict a castle from the worlds of fantasy, where there lurks a dragon and an old demon king, who is descending into madness and solitude. The artwork for their album *Castellum* features a solitary soldier who is guarding the entrance to a castle shrouded in mist; the group even go so far as to set an image of a castle in their logo. To display a fortified castle on an album cover is to show that you have a desire for grandeur; you flaunt your confidence in your own power, and

the image of the building aims to foreshadow the nobility of the music. But there is also a kind of nostalgia in displaying a structure that is today abandoned. Some of these fortresses have not withstood the ravages of time, and are now ruined, vanquished forever. The album sleeves of **Obsequiae** are a perfect illustration of the romantic ruin, imbued with a special aura combining grandeur and decline. What the castle loses in terror, it gains in melancholy. With *Visions from the Labyrinthine*, **Thuringwethil** opted for a ruin that appears out of the cold night, swallowed up by a dark forest. It does not take much for a castle to become a macabre emblem of the purest dark fantasy, a building where the blackest plots are hatched, a place very far from daylight – as in *Far Away from the Sun* by **Sacramentum**, who encircle their vampiric citadel with cliffs worthy of Moria. In an even more direct, minimalist style, **Lestrygon** display a medieval ruin in saturated black and white on the cover of *Mighty Kingdom of Darkness*, transforming the valiant castle into a demonic ruin. It is, after all, not surprising that these buildings appear mostly on black metal albums, whose music aims to be powerful, cavernous and dark, haunted like the moat of a forgotten castle whose master bays for blood.

Darkenhöld – *A Passage to the Towers*
Darkenhöld – *Castellum*
Sacramentum – *Far Away from the Sun*

A Passage To The Towers

Castellum

SACRAMENTUM

Far away from the Sun

In 1988, the group **Bathory** released *Blood Fire Death*, the cover for which featured the painting *The Wild Hunt of Odin* by Peter Nicolai Arbo. This album marks the transition between the group's purely speed black metal phase and a new period that is more melodic and atmospheric, but also more belligerent – **Manowar** having left their mark on **Quorthon**, the only permanent member of **Bathory**. There followed a whole series of albums based solely on the cult of his Scandinavian ancestors. Since then, Viking culture and the Viking aesthetic have occupied an important place in metal iconography, so powerfully does the perception of this culture speak to groups from northern Europe. The cultural region comprising the most groups that claim to be Viking metal is Scandinavia. It is a genre that is hard to define, and combines many different approaches. Some have moved away from traditional metal to flirt with folk music, whereas other groups consider themselves black metal or death metal, tinged with Viking etiquette, like the famous group **Amon Amarth**. This branch of metal imagines itself to be heroic, conquering music, as fascinating as a *drakkar* that emerges from the mist to approach your shores and plunder your villages (a symbol that **Turisas** use on *The Varangian Way*). However, the Viking way of life as a whole features on hundreds of album covers. They often show an armoured warrior in a natural setting, be it on water on in a forest, for this music is never very far from pagan metal or folk metal. Powerful warriors in symbiosis with nature; a life of clans, governed by certain values and a degree of martialism… all are features of the aura and values that metal sometimes likes to emanate. **HammerFall** even feature, as a recurring figure in their visuals, a Viking on horseback, brandishing the hammer Mjölnir as a call to war or a sign of victory. Other groups have completely built their whole visual world around idealized images of Viking culture. While **Ensiferum** emphasize heroic, warlike visuals, showing a soldier contemplating his homeland or exploring a frozen fjord, sword in hand, **Korpiklaani** opt for a sort of old bard with the look of a shaman, wearing a headdress of deer antlers, and holding a ritual drum. Finally, there are **Manilla Road** and their albums *Mark of the Beast* and *Voyager*, which take depictions of Vikings to the limit of heroic fantasy, showing the connections between Nordic culture and the supernatural.

Amon Amarth – *The Crusher*
Bathory – *Blood Fire Death*
Ensiferum – *Iron*
Bathory – *Hammerheart*

Lying outside any given folklore tradition, trees offer immeasurable symbolic scope. They grow for centuries and see humans come and go, put down roots in the earth, and are on first-name terms with the sky. They are the metaphor for rebirth and evolution, by virtue of photosynthesis, dead leaves that are transformed into humus, and the process of a seed becoming a great tree, thousands of years old. From the suicides transformed into gnarled trees in Dante's *Divine Comedy* to Tolkien's ents, trees have, unsurprisingly, been very popular with the creators of imaginary worlds. However, there is one that surpasses all others: Yggdrasil, the world tree of Nordic mythology, on which the Nine Worlds repose. **Darkened Winter** invite us on a journey through these with *Yggdrasil: Journey Throughout the Nine Worlds*. But this tree's epic aspect is more easily grasped from the album *Yggdrasil* by **Krilloan**, with its warrior setting off for an encounter with it, even though the cover simply shows a forest. For with this world tree, we are drawn into a web of legends and mythology. Despite its importance in Nordic myth, nothing is known about its origins except that it is the first tree of creation. It is a colossal, cosmic ash tree; one of its roots leads to Mimir, a figure that is the source of wisdom and memory, while another leads to Asgard, and a third leads to the kingdom of the dead. As **Dagor Bragollach** imply with *Cosmogony of Yggdrasil*, divine entities dwell within this gigantic tree. The great serpent Nidhogg gnaws at its roots, cursing a majestic eagle that lives on its highest branches. Ratatosk the squirrel shuttles back and forth, relaying the insults of each to the other, in perpetual equilibrium between the opposing forces. Legend tells that it was while suspended from one of its branches that Odin discovered the meaning of runes. This connection between runes and Yggdrasil is manifest on the cover of the album *Yggdrasil* by **Grívf**, which shows the mythical tree's name written in a runic typeface. Very often in metal, the

conclusion is a dark one: Yggdrasil is lost, as on the superb cover of *The Path* by the aptly-named **Ashes of Yggdrasil**, which depicts the world tree being consumed by flames in the distance. But the prize for the most impressive illustration goes unquestionably to **Kurgan**, with their *Yggdrasil Burns*, which shows a tree taller than the mountains, its roots exposed, and its leaves transformed into a cloud of flames. Yggdrasil easily found its way into pop culture. It features in the manga *Berserk*, in the novel *Hyperion* by Dan Simmons, and the video game *God of War*. Yggdrasil is the supreme tree of the world of the imagination.

Krilloan – *Yggdrasil*
Kurgan – *Yggdrasil Burns*
Darkened Winter – *Yggdrasil: Journey*
  Throughout the Nine Worlds

Egyptian and Sumerian culture – and, more broadly, all the civilisations that came into being in Mesopotamia – have folklore so rich and mystical that they go together perfectly with the imaginary world of metal. Oriental musical scales offer harmonies that lend themselves to mysterious riffs into which the tritone – the 'devil's interval' used in metal – fits easily. When accompanied by metal riffs, oriental harmonic structures produce a hypnotic, ancient-sounding aura, and lead more readily to a sort of trance. **Nile** are a concept group, all of whose albums revolve around ancient Egypt, its folklore and its gods. In a culture that comprised several strange deities and as many myths relating to the world of the dead, there is a great and inspiring wealth of themes for those who, like this group, are passionate about this historical period. This is clearly stated by the choice of visuals, as on the album *Those Whom the Gods Detest*, which features a stone pharaoh's head with a scarred face. The sleeve is distressed, as if timeworn, to convey subliminally that the album will carry the listener into the meanderings of a magnificent civilisation, now vanished. **Melechesh**, a black metal group from Israel, gravitate towards Sumerian folklore. Their album covers are tarnished with an old-fashioned sepia tint, and feature colossal sphinxes, menacing jinn, Babylonian statues and even, on their album *Emissaries*, the Tower of Babel. As the group's music proves, black metal can rise to the occasion when it comes to portraying this period, between history and myth, which saw the birth of civilisation. **Tamerlan Empire** go so far as to reference Tamerlane – the bloodthirsty warlord from what is now Uzbekistan, who presided over a military reign of terror – to embody their symphonic black metal and its Middle Eastern world. Posing in the desert wearing traditional dress reminiscent of that of Bedouins, this Australian group, whose drummer is Uzbek, clearly display their artistic direction. When a group is from one of these countries, the approach is slightly different, and doubtless more organic and visceral as well as less clichéd, than that of a Western group who adopt this style.

Akhenaten – *Incantations Through the Gates of Irkalla*
Melechesh – *Sphynx*
Melechesh – *Emissaries*
Nile – *Those Whom the Gods Detest*
Narjahanam – *Undama Tath'hur Al Shams Min Al Gharb* (When the Sun Descends from the West)
Tamerlan Empire – *Age of Ascendancy*

INCANTATIONS THROUGH THE GATES OF IRKALLA

SPHYNX

EMISSARIES

Since metal allows every culture its moment in the limelight, it is hardly surprising that there are groups that proclaim their fascination with Asian folklore. **Sigh**, pioneers of Japanese black metal and a spearhead of extreme metal and experimental metal in Japan, featured references to kabuki in their earliest artworks and borrowed from traditional painting of the feudal period, thus conveying the quaint, timeless nature of their music. Many Western groups also contributed to this trend. These include **Tokyo Blade**, representatives of the new wave of British heavy metal, and **Katana**, a group from the Swedish heavy metal revival. The vocalist/guitarist **Matt K. Heafy**, doubtless with the aim of paying homage to his roots on at least one album, dedicated the fourth by **Trivium** to the shoguns, military leaders of the Heian and feudal periods in Japan. Ideograms are used to spell out the album's name, and the edges of the cover feature intertwined Asian dragons. Even though China has seen fewer groups formed and received fewer references of this kind, it too has had its standard-bearers, and these – although of a more underground nature – are found in all branches of metal. **Black Kirin**, for example, behind those paintings of majestic Chinese landscapes, conceal a melodic death metal with hints of traditional music. Mongolia was not to be outdone, as demonstrated by the recent passion for **The Hu**, who enrich their modern metal with diphonic singing and traditional instruments. In a less flashy style, **Tengger Cavalry** convey, through their large number of records, their love of Tengrism, shamanism and Central Asian nomad cultures, always conveyed by visuals in which horses and traditional dress are at the fore. As for **Nine Treasures**, their name references the nine materials described in ancient Mongolian poetry. Here too, traditional instruments, such as the morin khuur and the Jew's harp, combine with saturated guitars and drums. In its most modern branches, metal has managed to pay homage to more contemporary cultures. One part of Asian culture that has travelled particularly well outside the continent's borders is manga, and many young Westerners were able to make it their own when it began to be imported on a massive scale in the 1980s. Two French groups in particular showed a keen interest

in Japanese animated films and strip cartoons. For their album *Medecine Cake*, **Pleymo** – a flagship nu metal group of the 2000s – came up with a whole artistic direction inspired by mangas, for which their vocalist/frontman **Mark Maggiori** was an enthusiast. For the tour of this album, each musician wore an outfit of a different single colour, in the style of *Super Sentai* (more familiar to many as *Mighty Morphin Power Rangers*). Today, it is the hardcore metal group **Rise of the Northstar**, who play the shonen manga card to the full and appropriate certain Japanese cultural codes, going as far as to wear the *gakuran* (Japanese school uniform) on stage, or outfits worn by the Bōsōzoku, a Japanese bikers' gang. Injecting metal into a culture often has the effect of bringing out its dark, heroic and fascinating side.

Sigh – *Ghastly Funeral Theatre*
Sigh – *Scorn Defeat*

It is a little-known fact that, in folk metal, there are many groups that make use of the aesthetic and themes linked to the Aztec and Maya cultures. When extreme music groups – in this case, chiefly black metal – claim to be followers of a certain historical period and explore the fantasies it generates, it is often in order to pay homage to cultures that have since vanished and bear the strong hallmarks of a warlike, mystical ideal. This doubtless explains the nationalistic slant of many of these groups, as with any movement that references ancient cultures by fantasizing about them in order to imagine it is descended from something superiorw. Most of these groups' names are in the Mayan or Aztec languages, thus creating a connection to the tradition and memory of the culture they seek to celebrate. The real and imagined folklore of these cultures is so rich in visions and symbols that it is not surprising to see it adopted by metal. The stepped pyramid is at the centre of most of the album covers of **Xibalba**, who have often called on the genius of Dan Seagrave, whose art manages to arouse a morbid fascination when faced with the grandeur of these structures. **Xibalba** is, incidentally, the Maya name for the underground world

ruled by the deities of death and disease. Sometimes the pyramid is juxtaposed with our contemporary society in almost apocalyptic visions, as in the case of **MaYaN** and **Destination Void**. The idea of the end of time is strongly associated with this culture, both because of the Maya calendar and because of the sudden, mysterious disappearance of their civilization. To refer to Maya pyramids is also to remind us that ancient, all-powerful worlds collapsed long before we were on the scene, and that perhaps that fate awaits us too. Other groups, such as **Volahn**, **Tunjum**, and **Impureza**, highlight the sacrificial aspect of certain rites and offerings to the gods. Some deities are given pride of place, as in the case of the group **Death Karma**, who show the deity Kukulkan – the equivalent of the Aztecs' Quetzalcoatl – inside their first album. Finally, taking a different approach, other groups such as **Sepultura** have tried a form of return to the sources, to the roots, with their album *Roots* drawing its anger from the tribal energy of jungle peoples.

Impureza – *La Caída de Tonatiuh* (The Fall of Tonatiuh)
MaYaN – *Quarterpast*

If metal often makes use of cultural and historical references, it is because that makes a direct connection with imaginary worlds that are firmly fixed in the collective unconscious: a knight in armour alone is enough to evoke the Middle Ages. Similarly, to adopt symbols of piracy as a group identity, and to feature aspects of buccaneering, carries us to a world highly charged with codes and legends. The figure of the pirate evokes the complete freedom of someone who is unfettered by the laws of society. He has his own language, made up of slang and colourful expressions. He plunders, sails the seas, and sinks hostile ships. He hoists his skull-and-crossbones flag to notify the world of his gruesome intentions. Although pirates are depicted as bloodthirsty brutes lured by profit and devoid of values, that seems to be far from the truth. They also had a code of honour and sharing, their aim being to live on the margins of society rather than to destroy it. Despite everything, the idealized image of a godless and lawless Blackbeard is an enduring one, and metal does not shrink from conjuring it up. Pirate metal is often heroic, lively heavy metal. It is easy to imagine a menacing ship emerging from a stormy horizon to the sound of *Under Jolly Roger* by **Running Wild** or *Return to Port Royal* by **Blazon Stone**. *Port Royal* is also the theme and title of another album by **Running Wild**, an homage to the British government's port in Jamaica, which was home to pirates in their time. In this way, the two groups demonstrate their common perception of buccaneering, and mine the same seam of the imagination, whose themes conform perfectly to the world of metal. The figure of the pirate sweeps us away into tales of maps revealing buried treasure, as well as hidden galleons, endless feasts and merciless attacks at sea. He brings a whiff of ocean spray and danger; he is elusive. The artwork of *Hoist the Black Flag* by

Iron SeaWolf uses the image of an old leather and gold book of lore, which contains some riddle that leads us to treasures hidden in trading posts in a tropical paradise, or on secret islands. In the cases of both **Running Wild** and *Pilgrimage* by **Zed Yago**, the pirate also evokes the idea of brotherhood, a crew, people bound to life and death by a wild love of freedom and adventure – which, after all, fits rather well with the destiny of a group of musicians who launch themselves into the great epic of metal.

Iron SeaWolf – *Hoist the Black Flag*
Running Wild – *Under Jolly Roger*
Zed Yago – *Pilgrimage*

IRON SEAWOLF

HOIST THE BLACK FLAG

RUNNING WILD

Under Jolly Roger

ZED YAGO

PILGRIMAGE

Earth has been nicknamed the Blue Planet because so much of its surface is covered by water. Seas and oceans represent a great expanse to be explored, and their depths are such a source of mystery that a voyage can arouse fear as well as a kind of fascination. Although humans are still very far from having explored all that lies in the ocean deep, they send out stellar probes hundreds of thousands of kilometres from Earth, and seek to colonize some corners of the solar system. It is indeed technologically more feasible to venture into the heavens than to probe the depths of our own planet. This great unknown, and its unfathomable darkness, are the source of certain myths and legends, such as the lost empire of Atlantis, the Leviathan in the Bible, and the myth of the Cthulhu. The group **Atlantis Chronicles** took the decision to centre their career on marine exploration and nautical fantasies, even going so far as to include a narrator on their second album, *Barton's Odyssey*, to heighten the sense of immersion. The album revisits the life of Otis Barton, a pioneer, a deep-sea diver and the author of *The World Beneath the Sea*, a book about submarine exploration. As for stories about the oceans, the nautical funeral doom metal of **Ahab** takes us off to hunt Moby Dick, the white whale of Herman Melville's novel, as well as to drift on the raft from the painting *The Raft of the Medusa*, or to descend into the depths of the ocean in order to encounter weird, multicoloured sea creatures. **Mastodon**, on their album *Leviathan*, also feature a highly distinctive account of the hunt for the big white cachalot. Flamboyant visuals, explicit lyrics and a musical atmosphere that fits perfectly with what the songs relate – all is geared to making us experience the adventure to the full alongside Captain Ahab, the man with the ivory leg. Although the blue surface that separates us from the black abyss below can appear smooth and soothing, that all changes when a storm brews, as Japanese band **Blaze** show us with their first album. Once we have cast off, we take the risk of coming face to face with the unpredictability of water – which, like all the other elements, becomes a formidable threat if it is not mastered. Metal is like the storm that causes boats to dance in a watery ballet that is chaotic and deadly. That, at any rate, is what is suggested by many groups' artworks, which show small boats buffeted by waves that seem to want

to devour them. More broadly, the ocean is also synonymous with infinity and abundance, which contrasts with its other, more unpredictable and cruel aspects. It seems to be alive, to have its own personality and changes of mood, as if it were a being in its own right. It is surely for all these reasons that the word 'ocean' recurs so often in the titles of songs and albums, and even the names of groups. Artists who make use of this powerful, suggestive marine iconography aim in this way to emphasize the diverse, contrasting aspect of their music. What is more evocative than a mariner in the thick of a storm who, looking Neptune straight in the eye, confronts the elements as he faces his destiny?

Ahab – *The Boats of the Glen Carrig*

Atlantis Chronicles – *Barton's Odyssey*

Ahab – *The Call of the Wretched Sea*

Ahab – *The Divinity of Oceans*

WAR

As **Nargaroth** proclaim with the title of the album *Black Metal Ist Krieg*, 'black metal is war'. The group illustrate this statement by posing with a weapon in each hand, ready to do battle with anyone who tries to contradict them. Black metal's war is a battle against the world and against divine light, a fight against itself and others. Murderous armed conflict is undeniably an inspiration for these artists, whether they seek to denounce it or to replay the feelings it arouses through music. When metal dons its darkest garb, it is not there to say good things or point out beautiful ones: it seeks to stir up the darkness and turn it into a fuel, be it cathartic or nihilistic. The madness of war gives humans a feeling of power and impunity. In times of war we sometimes see the best – but always the worst. On *…For Victory*, **Bolt Thrower** try to beautify conflict by depicting soldiers silhouetted against the setting sun, fighting for an ideal. With **Justabeli**, who come under the war black metal category, it is the opposite: on the cover of *Satanic War Black Metal*, the powerful people of the world are seated around a table and eat human bones while making a pact with the demon of war, who

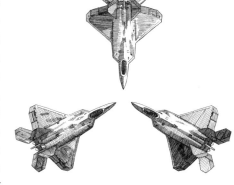

appears here in the shape of Baphomet, armed to the teeth. Besides the decision-makers, there are of course the soldiers themselves, who are capable of selling their values cheaply to indulge in the most dreadful inhumanity. This is portrayed on the sleeve of *Street War Metal Kommand*, a split album by **Abigail** and **Hate Kommand**. The uniforms no longer clothe humans, but barbaric skeletons with empty eye sockets, which drive over the debris of pillaged, devastated towns and give themselves over to the worst atrocities, laughing. War is a wonderful playground for anyone who wants to depict all that is worst about humanity. And the world of metal loves to raise the stakes, so it is not surprising that armed conflict, a sign of

the failure of human beings to resolve their differences, is such a source of inspiration for this musical genre. War can, incidentally, be easily combined with worlds that are more mythological or even from science fiction. The cover of the album *Battle Breed* by **Bodyfarm** flirts with *Mad Max* and the games *Fallout* and *Killzone*, while **Vader** speak bluntly of the art of war in a futuristic dystopia, showing a robot setting off to fight, as if to say that the violence of war will remain undiminished, and will progress despite the passage of time. Death metal is the ideal soundtrack to illustrate the fury of a tank, the shock of a cannon's explosion. Guttural, animal-like vocals call to mind the roar of a military leader yelling at his troops to galvanize them into action. The firepower and precision of this music could make an unmotivated soldier want to fight, charging him with destructive energy so that he rushes headlong towards chaos.

Bodyfarm – *Battle Breed*

Split Abigail / Hate Kommand – *StreetWar Metal Kommand*

Nargaroth – *Black Metal Ist Krieg*

Turisas - *Battle Metal*

Although the 20th century brought its fair share of marvels and progress, it also saw two world wars devastate entire regions. While war has always been a horror, with these two conflicts it attained heights of barbarism that still haunt us today. During the First World War, from 1914 to 1918, it was chiefly the nightmare of the trenches and their consequences, such as facially mutilated war veterans, that would inspire artists. There are powerful reasons to tell the story of the fate of these sacrificed soldiers, who were sent in their thousands into battles that it was known in advance would be lost. That is exactly what **FT-17** do on *Marcellin s'en va-t'en guerre* (Marcellin Goes to War), which features on its cover a ghostlike soldier on a battlefield reeking of death and despair. In contrast to this melancholy, almost contemplative approach, **Heresiarch**'s *Death Ordinance* depicts the infernal darkness of these conflicts – and all with a graphic touch reminiscent of traditional classical painting. On *The Great War*, **Sabaton** opt for a spectacular but tragic portrayal featuring a soldier amid the chaos of the trenches, covering his bleeding eyes with his hands. The First World War saw the

birth of warfare that was technological and industrial, inhuman by its very nature: bombs and shells, grenades and poison gas, tanks, rotary guns and other machines of death. In these, metal finds as much to glorify as it does to abhor. On the one hand, there is the bravery of the soldier, who goes to drive out the army of evil, as in the case of **ShadowKiller** and their album *Until the War is Won*, which depicts GIs beating a Nazi soldier who has just been dragged from his tank. On the other hand, the sleeve of *Operation Wintersturm* by **Endstille** portrays the nihilistic darkness of war by means of a photographic negative of a razed village, covered in graves. But it is the Second World War that provided really fertile ground for the imagination of

certain groups, even if this served as a pretext for conveying Nazi political views using artistic creativity as a cover. It is always in black metal that we see this fine line being trodden. Although the boundary is blurred in some cases (and very clear in others), it is a period that is often revisited by those who seek to explore the blackness of the human soul. As *Campo de Exterminio* (Extermination Camp) by the group **Holocausto** shows, during that war, humanity experienced evil in its pure state, and the horrors perpetrated by the Nazis plunged us into a morbid vision of what humans are capable of. It is not surprising that these dark historical times are invoked by groups that ceaselessly question our inner monstrousness.

FT-17 – *Marcellin s'en va-t'en guerre*

Endstille – *Operation Wintersturm*

Sabaton – *The Great War*

ShadowKiller – *Until the War is Won*

The Cold War is the historical period that saw the birth of rock, hard rock and metal. The tensions and trauma that it caused are written into the genetic code of rock and the subgenres that grew out of it. The hippie movement originated in part from the protests against the Vietnam War and against the West's military policy in general. That is how the protest songs of 1960s folk rock came into being. Artists such as **Bob Dylan**, **Joan Baez** and **Jimi Hendrix** opposed armed conflict and supported civil rights both in their songs and, in some cases, their daily lives. This anti-establishment, protesting attitude was part of the ideological foundations of a rock scene that was in full ferment – and Woodstock was its high point. At the same time, the Space Race suggested to the world that there could be life beyond our planet, a reality that merged with fiction. The sky, space and extraterrestrial travel fuelled the dreams of many musicians who had come from the psychedelic rock and progressive rock scenes, such as **Pink Floyd** and **Tangerine Dream**. That is how space rock came into being. But, beyond the Cold War itself and its collateral damage – which proved to be real tragedies – this period was also marked by the coldness and austerity of the Communist bloc. This atmosphere made an impression on the trend of industrial music that emerged at the end of the 1970s, and also on that of much more recent metal groups, such as **Kursk**. The cover of their first album, *Cherno*, suggests all the architectural austerity of the Soviet world. Above the group's logo there shines a big red star in a grey sky. Where trauma did not give way to far-right, neo-Nazi tendencies, some groups in Eastern European countries opted instead for anti-Communism or anti-Stalinism. The Cold War also saw the arms race and the development of nuclear power. Thrash metal clearly conveys all the suspicion regarding the nuclear escalation fuelled by the Cold War, which the Chernobyl accident did nothing to help. On the cover of *Game Over*, **Nuclear Assault** portray a city and its inhabitants completely burned to ashes by a nuclear explosion, while in a more extreme and industrial

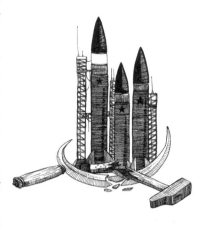

style, the French group **Art 238** released, in 2002, a demo featuring a track entitled 'One Day in Tchernobyl', its lyrics filled with nuclear terminology. The arrival of perestroika following Gorbachev's coming to power, and the subsequent fall of the Berlin Wall, were a relief for the whole of Europe. **Scorpions** sang of this relief in 'Wind of Change' on the album *Crazy World*. The many themes raised by the Cold War and its duration mean that the entirety of its influence is as vast as it is unfathomable.

Kursk – *Cherno*
Sodom – *Agent Orange*

It is not unusual to hear music critics who specialize in extreme music use terminology relating to heaviness and power to describe a group's style: 'A massive album, with heavy, overwhelming sounds, which creates the effect of a steamroller…' One imagines a helpless listener, floored by what they have just heard. Where war, good and evil, the military aesthetic and death intersect, there is the tank. An avatar of modern, mechanized warfare, a tank on an album cover expresses not only self-conscious virility that wants to appear triumphant, but also the conquering, merciless spirit of the music it heralds. This is illustrated literally on the cover of *The Return of the Filth Hounds* by the aptly named group **Tank**, for the vehicle is pictured bursting directly out of a speaker, thus expressing the effect the music is meant to produce. *Panzer Division Marduk* by **Marduk** contains music of unheard-of violence, on an album that points its cannon directly at the listener. The tank feeds into a military aesthetic that is as warlike as it is unhealthy, and which infuses the music with the smell of sulphur and smoke. Indeed, groups themselves do all they can to make this war machine into an evil instrument, a sign of political forces that have become mad and send 'unstoppable' machines to massacre entire cities. In this sense, the tank is infernal. **Angelcorpse** named their album *Exterminate*; it depicts surreal-looking tanks in various forms, made of flesh and steel, accompanied by legions from hell, and driving over thousands of bodies. These images are all the stronger because, though imaginary, they convey perfectly the horrors of war. To feature a tank on an album cover is political in itself, anti-establishment, and sometimes in questionable taste (that is, when it is not in outright bad taste, such as on the sleeve of *Heavy Metal Tank* by **Metalucifer**, which shows the group's mascot, Tanaka, emerging from a tank that is crushing

people who represent what he detests). In other instances, the tank is glorified as a satanic symbol used for blasphemy, its cannon viewed as a phallic object and a tool for desecration. Sometimes it even transports Baphomet and his ghouls, as on the cover of *Trumpets of Triumph* by **Godless Rising**, where it is the crucified Christ himself who is placed on the tank by way of a trophy. Metal has many faces, but the tank perfectly assumes its head-on heaviness, for here it is less a matter of showing subtlety than of a barbaric, cathartic explosion of sound. In this sense, the tank is the ideal metaphor for this desire to assault the listener's eardrums and mind, as the cover of *War Without End* by **Warbringer** shows so well; the group's very name shows their hand, promising a sound that 'brings war'.

Tank – *The Return of the Filth Hounds*
Godless Rising – *Trumpet of Triumph*
Marduk – *Panzer Division Marduk*
Warbringer – *War Without End*

CLAVES CIVITATIS

THE KEYS TO THE CITY

SPRAY PAINT

Given metal's origins, it may have seemed unlikely that it would incorporate street culture and aesthetics, but today it seems obvious that it has. While groups such as **Rage Against the Machine** turned the spotlight on the fusion of metal and hip-hop, the whole of nu metal embraced this hybrid culture. The guitar parts of **Korn** are often conceived as samples, and the 'slap' bass guitar is reminiscent of a kind of cavernous funk; **Limp Bizkit** have in their line-up a DJ from the hip-hop scene; and **Slipknot** are closer to a masked gang than to a group of conventional musicians… The cover of Limp Bizkit's *Three Dollar Bill,Yall$* is drawn in felt-tip pen, in a very b-boy style, while that of *Significant Other* shows a graffiti-style **Fred Durst**. There are many examples of this hybridization of street culture and metal. On the cover of *Meteora*, **Linkin Park** capture a graffiti artist, spray can in hand, creating his work, while **Enhancer** hide the title of their album *Street Trash* in a discreet tag hidden on a wall, at the same time paying homage to the discipline of parkour. Hardcore metal groups have also exalted this culture of graffiti and tags, the style often being closely related to the urban culture of skateboarding. The title of the album *Hardcore Lives* by **Madball** is shown as a tag on the metal roller door of a warehouse, and the artwork of the logo on the album *Promo '17* by **Worst Doubt** makes a connection between graffiti, street wear and hardcore metal. The toughness of street culture fits perfectly with angry riffs and screaming singing. The practice of graffiti is itself a spirit and discipline that pairs well with music that bursts with urgency and adrenalin. Painting graffiti is against the law and forces the artist to take risks, trespass and leave their mark on urban surfaces that are meant to be immaculate. While some see this as an act of vandalism, others see it as a noble art. Countercultures adopt similar mechanisms, and it is not surprising that music is one of the links between activities that are not part of the system. **Suicidal Tendencies** show this well on *The Art of Rebellion*, which depicts the *Mona Lisa* on fire, with the album title tagged on the wall of the museum like a slogan, making a statement. Graffiti is an art that imposes itself on the concrete in which people are drowning. This is why people talk about 'street art'. Furthermore, the graffiti tag conveys ideas of territory, identity and secret codes – it is a language all its own, which is literally written on the walls in the street. Sometimes, that means symbolizing the dark, murderous side, as in the case of the album *Cold Street Homicide*, which bears the logo of the group **Machete 187** in the form of white graffiti on a wall – 187 being gang code for murder. No need to show anything more: one graffito sums up all the harshness of this group's music and their world.

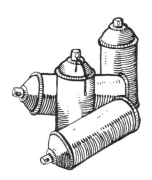

Enhancer – *Street Trash*
Worst Doubt – *Promo '17*
Machete 187 – *Cold Street Homicide*

In a form of *mise en abyme* (a story within a story), many groups feature on their album covers the metal fan in their natural habitat. Most often, in heavy metal or thrash metal, they are a male, unshaven thirty-something with long hair, dressed in leather, jeans or a jacket covered in patches that glorify their favourite group. These images often verge on parody of 1980s thrasher metal, just like Tanaka, the improbable mascot of **Metalucifer**. Most of the artworks are drawings or paintings rather than photographs, in the style beloved of *Mad Magazine* and *Métal Hurlant*, and you can almost recognize a group just by their album sleeves. To discover thrash metal around the age of 15 makes you take a different direction and plunges you into a world that can change you. This is beautifully conveyed on the cover of *Beware of Metal* by the group **IntoxXxicateD**, which depicts metal as a no-go area which you enter to experience thrills and to position yourself on the margins of society: the metalhead lifestyle. **Violator** makes it a guiding principle with the cover of *Violent Mosh*, which shows stage diving during a concert by the group on the front, and fans queuing outside the venue on the back. The use of coloured crayons for the visuals gives it the do-it-yourself look of a fanzine or of a drawing done in an exercise book while not paying attention in class. A bottle of spirits, a cigarette and a patched jacket – the rock and roll lifestyle also acts as a social connection. It brings with it a state of mind that prioritizes freedom and taking things to extremes. Metal becomes part of one's lifestyle, and all these album covers reflect back to listeners an image of themselves, which heightens the sense of belonging. In this vein, the album *Thrash Metal Victory* by **Traitor** shows a close-up of a denim jacket that displays patches of groups that Traitor's members themselves idolize, as if to say that, before becoming musicians, they were fans first of all. In other cases, the group themselves appear

centre stage, to depict the unvarnished, direct side of their approach to life, and show they are like their fans. That is what **Exodus** do on *Fabulous Disaster*, which shows the group's members in a room, drinking beer in front of the television. But not all groups promote such a good-natured image. When they come to town, metalheads know how to be more threatening, and they can become oafish, even delinquent hoodlums. Thrash metal is an urban music genre that has a strong atmosphere of dark back alleys and street fights. The music must sound like a threat and the visual must be its emissary. **Fueled by Fire** ratchet this up further with *Spread the Fire*, an ode to criminality, pure and simple, in the style of *A Clockwork Orange*. In a more hard rock vein, **Electric Shock** opt for a squalid, brazen vision of a city filled with vice in *Trapped in the City*.

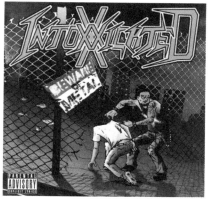

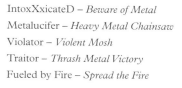

IntoxXxicateD – *Beware of Metal*
Metalucifer – *Heavy Metal Chainsaw*
Violator – *Violent Mosh*
Traitor – *Thrash Metal Victory*
Fueled by Fire – *Spread the Fire*

ULTRA-VIOLENCE

In metal's tumultuous galaxy, raising the stakes is very often an essential element: one must always go further, and to do worse is highly thought of… Here too, this bloodstained extreme is meant to symbolize the music, and it promises a symphony of ultra-violence. It gives an idea of the aggressiveness of sound and the nasty feelings of which it is the ambassador. Music has the power to affect your body and emotions, and metal is capable of literally overcoming you and making you throw yourself completely into listening. Extreme music groups have always tried to push back the boundaries of morality and taboo in order to arouse curiosity and fear, giving their music an extra aura of the macabre. This skilful blend, which comes straight from horror and exploitation films – as demonstrated by the visuals of **National Suicide** on *Massacre Elite* and **Frightmare** on *Midnight Murder Mania* – nevertheless reaches peaks of violence that are rarely attained. Indeed, of all formats, and far more so than comics, metal album covers are unquestionably where the most disturbing and outrageous images in all of the history of art are found. From its beginnings, metal has been seen as dangerous, deviant music by some conservative institutions, and it seems that bands have done all they can to continue to be worthy of this reputation. On the cover of *First Class Violence*, **Darkness** revisit the aesthetic of the violent thug who prowls the ravaged city, ready to beat you up, while Anal Cunt go for simplicity with a photo of a man in a rage hitting another on the cover of an album with the evocative title *Everyone Should Be Killed*. But the commonest theme is probably that of the barbaric apocalypse, where the streets are invaded by bloodthirsty hordes that make Alex DeLarge of *A Clockwork Orange* look like a gentle lamb. **Disgruntled Anthropophagi** express this shocking visual energy with the title of their album

Rampage of Misanthropic Purge. It is frequently anger and disgust with humanity that shape the vocabulary of these groups. Despite the disturbing gore aspect, the whole is often salvaged by a style that is close to that of comics, which prevents the crossing of the line of what cannot be shown, as is sometimes done by goregrind. This art style, somewhere between painting and airbrushing, is so pregnant with adolescent fantasy and the culture of the 1980s that it has produced some visuals that, in theory, should be absolutely atrocious but in the hands of an artist become quite simply cathartic and captivating.

Cranium – *Speed Metal Sentence*
Sudden Rage – *Blind Trust*

CONCRETE

Hell can take on different appearances, and beyond the red flames of the Judaeo-Christian limbo, all kinds of different visions of Hell have made an impression on artists as a means of expressing the nightmare that existence makes them experience. The urban blight of dormitory cities is an example as unexpected as it is powerful. The excessive urbanization of our planet, and the 1960s utopian vision of living together – which consisted of building rows of gigantic tower blocks – have produced angst for the human beings that survive there. The first feelings experienced when enduring these concrete colossi on a daily basis are suffocation, a sense of injustice and anger. So it is not surprising to find visuals of depressing cities shown in black-and-white photographs in the work of beatdown hardcore groups with elements of street culture, who want to show the bleakness of life at the foot of these tower blocks. The group **Words of Concrete** perfectly capture this imaginary world with the title of their album *East German Cold*. The evocation of the part of Berlin that was under Soviet control corresponds well to the austerity they seek to convey. These brutal-looking apartment blocks are a sign of oppression, and any hint of *joie de vivre* is absent from these images. The concrete is grey, dreary, hard. On *Curb Games Re-Visited*, the group **In Blood We Trust** moves up a notch, showing a ghetto surrounded by barbed wire whose sinister blocks are reflected in puddles of water. In this same dark, rundown style, **On a Warpath** and **Hypomanie** opt on their eponymous albums for a special effect on the theme of time, showing images of modern cities shot using a photographic technique from the beginning of the 20th century, as if these places have been erased from historical memory – as if people were trying to forget them. **Shattered Realm** say it all, indicating where their music is coming from with the title of their album *From the Dead End Blocks Where Life Means*

Nothing. Another feeling that emanates from these concrete fortresses is despair tinged with fatalism. There is a point in common with hip-hop and rap artists here: mixing their emotions through their music, using language whose codes come from the street and working-class neighbourhoods. The angst of megalopolises manages to become even more desperate in the depressive suicidal black metal of **Aurora Disease**. On the cover of *Burial of Self* is a threatening dormitory city photographed from a low angle, standing out against a dark night. On all these covers, there is never a single human figure: they have vanished from the landscape, hiding away and suffering in silence inside the concrete blocks.

Aurora Disease – *Burial of Self*
Lifelover – *Dekadens*

Industrial music provides everything its name promises. A musical style in its own right, it aims to create a sound-space that is reminiscent of that of factories and their metallic cacophony – the repetition of hard, cold sounds made by the sharp movements of inhuman machine tools, hammering out their implacable rhythm. The album covers of **Fear Factory** perfectly convey this atmosphere, and revolve around a noxious fusion between machines and humans, in a biomechanical approach worthy of H. R. Giger. Their album *Demanufacture* shows us a barcode that is transformed into a ribcage, while *Digimortal* shows a human figure trapped in a computer's motherboard... Industrial music has sometimes taken highly experimental and 'noise music' approaches, as in the case of the German group **Einstürzende Neubauten**, who use building site machinery to make their music. Subsequently, industrial metal did all it could to conjure up the deathly, urban aspect of our ultra-mechanized society – as if a demonic power lurked in the inhuman march of the world. The visual aesthetic of these groups fits perfectly with the musical content: drum machines, repetitive, hypnotic loops, and massive distortion of syncopated, precise guitars. As for the lyrics, they describe a cold world in which human warmth is only a vague idea. The group **KMFDM**, for their part, have opted for covers whose graphics are reminiscent of Soviet propaganda posters, to drive home the martial and almost totalitarian aspect of this style of music. **Ministry** have made this their guiding principle with regards to visuals, featuring covers that are anti-establishment and morbid, with an almost conspiratorial aesthetic. Unwholesome patriotism, dishonest politicians who have sold our world to corporations: society itself is an oppressive machine. For their graphics, **Static-X** opted for cold, computer-like 3D visuals, while

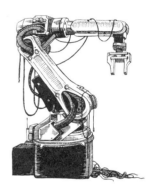

Filter feature medicine packaging... Anything connected to mass consumption and the alienation it brings with it suits the genre well. The album *City* by **Strapping Young Lad** shows a diagram of a machine in place of a city plan, as if we are merely replaceable components in a great mechanism. The sleeve of the album *Add Violence* by **Nine Inch Nails** features a close-up photo of a factory's control panel. In the end, it is **Front Line Assembly** who are at the intersection of all these aesthetics, and who make the link between industrialization and our dissolution as humans within that system. Their album *Fallout* and its striking visual – a human face attached to a pistol cartridge that looks like a rocket – says a lot about the aesthetic that runs through this trend in music.

KMFDM – *Attak*
Strapping Young Lad – *City*
Ministry – *Filth Pig*

While it is clear that a good part of the metal scene is reluctant to announce its political ideas, there are nevertheless some subgenres that are known for being politically committed and for accepting a militant dimension in their music. While many groups have played with the tools of political propaganda used by 20th-century totalitarian regimes, this has often been for aesthetic reasons, or to create a controversy for commercial gain at the lowest possible cost. But in the punk hardcore and crust movements, there are a number of visual signals that come from alternative circles. The cover of *The Day the Country Died* by **Subhumans** has a whiff of the fanzine about it, and some of the energy of self-produced punk comics. The visual statement and the album's title are direct and committed: it shows a rebellious punk throwing a Molotov cocktail in the midst of a demonstration, standing between a priest and a police officer, while bombs rain down from the sky. Between them, various albums cover all the big, classic themes of social struggle. On *Point Blank*, **Nailbomb** throw the horror and cruelty of war right in our faces with a photo of an old woman being held at gunpoint. The same can be said for the album *War Crimes Inhuman Beings* by **Doom**, which shows the corpse of a victim of war. Through the use of images that are so shocking and so distressing to look at, we feel that the group have taken a position of anger and will make us aware, through their music, of the horror of the world in which we live. The American nuclear family, traditional and conservative, also comes in for criticism, most notably by **Black Flag** with their visual for *Family Man*. The layout of these album covers and their often minimalist design, lacking complacent aesthetic pretensions, conveys a kind of urgency and lack of resources, a 'do-it-yourself' energy and a desire for independence. They often come close to a political pamphlet pure and simple: the cover of *You Are One* by **Unity** is a good example of this, with its angry figure breaking

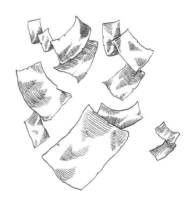

down a brick wall made up of all the themes he is fighting against. Music has always accompanied politics, but it has also fuelled it. The further they are from the mainstream, the more musicians feel entitled to express political opinions. The cover of *One Voice* by the group **Agnostic Front** is typical of these albums: its use of journalistic photography makes us feel that the record serves a cause or a struggle rather than merely the desire to make music. Now, music is such a powerful emotional medium that it can convey ideas and an energy that are the envy of our politicians.

Black Flag – *Family Man*

Unity – *You are One*

Subhumans – *The Day the Country Died*

Nailbomb – *Point Blank*

TOXIC

Just as war is a source of artistic inspiration, so too can disasters have influence on the collective unconscious. Although monsters such as Godzilla were created in a Japan that was trying to exorcize the tragedy of two atomic bombs, the rest of the world did not wait for such tragic events to happen before exploring the nuclear nightmare. It is on the thrash metal scene that the dangers of this technology are represented the most. While some groups took an almost realistic approach – such as **Nuclear Assault** with *The Plague*, which openly refers to the Chernobyl disaster – album covers have usually looked to genre films rather than to militant tracts. The B-movie aspect of some covers is reminiscent of cult low-budget films from Troma Entertainment such as *The Toxic Avenger*, the story of a failed high-school student who transforms himself into a radioactive mutant and takes revenge on those who harassed him. The freedom of these movies – reminiscent of punk and gore – goes perfectly with the world that thrash metal has been able to call its own. The cover of *Unnatural Selection* by **Havok** looks at the worrying manipulation by humans of dangerous substances, featuring a scientist who is portrayed as a mad scholar resembling Dr Frankenstein. Yet, at the close of a Cold War that almost plunged the world into chaos, it was no longer so much the atomic bomb that was frightening as it was nuclear power itself, which posed a Promethean risk to health. Despite the teasing visuals on the covers of pulp magazines and comics, the fears relating to this new threat are expressed directly. With the EP *The Last Rager*, **Municipal Waste** depict a 'zombified' world, plunged into a nuclear apocalypse that takes us back to the state of savage cannibals. Their split EP with **Toxic Holocaust**, entitled *Toxic Waste*, highlights the inherent connection between body horror and nuclear contamination, an ideal tableau for an aggressive,

overpowering style of metal, reinforced by urgent, incisive riffs. The whole vocabulary of waste, toxicity and nuclear power is featured, and corresponds perfectly with the spectre of a nuclear war. On *High on Radiation*, **Reactory** portray a desolate trench alongside a zombie soldier, high on radiation, on the point of putting on his gas mask. In the nuclear aesthetic of thrash metal, the almost ever-present graphic connecting thread is fluorescent green. From *The Simpsons'* opening credits to the movie *Re-Animator*, bright green substances have always been the symbol of the forbidden experiment, the radioactive material that irradiates with its invisible poison. The fluorescence literally jumps out at us, and is a rallying symbol for the toxic, post-Chernobyl generation: it hangs over the gloom and the blown-up concrete, like the swansong of a civilization that nuclear winter will soon extinguish.

Municipal Waste x Toxic Holocaust – *Toxic Waste*
Reactory – *High on Radiation*

The caricature of elites is a recurrent motif in the speed metal, thrash metal and death metal scenes, and it is often the brush of the great Ed Repka that has brought the most memorable of these illustrations to life. The approach is often the same: depict a ruling caste in the middle of an apocalyptic scene. These are sometimes evangelical Christians or priests, as on the covers of *Spiritual Healing* by **Death** and *Twisted Prayers* by **Gruesome**. The man of God is seen as a manipulator surrounded by blinded sheep. Politicians are not spared, and are portrayed as dictators who extol a religion based on power and money, hidden behind an altar of death. Their two-faced, lying side is criticized in the artwork of *Two-Faced* by **Tankard**. Sometimes politicians are shown in a worse position, because the time has come to pay for their crimes. **Angelus Apatrida** invoke the revolutionary spirit in their *Cabaret de la guillotine* (Guillotine Cabaret), while **Sodom** fantasize about a war against dishonest elites, showing their soldier-mascot unmasking and grabbing the rulers of the world on the cover of *Masquerade in Blood*. In the cases of **D.R.I.** on *Dealing with It!* and **Toxik** on *Think This*, it is the people themselves who are shown in a negative light: consumerist, blinded by the lies on television, and submissive to the system, as if this world renders us mad and passive at the same time. For behind every politician, there hides a businessman, who dictates his financial imperatives and who holds the powerful of this world in the palm of his hand. On *For Whose Advantage?*, **Xentrix** show us a trader with a predatory smile in front of the gleaming towers of a business district with an atmosphere reminiscent of the movie *American Psycho*. The Hong Kong group **Charm Charm Chu** share the same language, depicting, on the cover of *Majestic Brewing Order*, a financier with the head of a pig who is preparing to launch a new brand of beer like a missile. With **Hyades**, finally, the idea is a more general one, with a human being in the throes of

mutation, surfing a wave that is engulfing our civilization – and the album's title, *And The Worst Is Yet To Come*, says a lot about the violence of the satire found in thrash metal, which comes close to the 'no future' idea espoused by punk in its time. These album covers, as satirical as they are fascinating, are perfect hybrids of the political cartoon and the horror film poster.

Charm Charm Chu – *Majestic Brewing Order*
Sodom – *Masquerade in Blood*
Angelus Apatrida – *Cabaret de la guillotine*
Xentrix – *For Whose Advantage?*
Tankard – *Two-Faced*
Toxik – *Think This*

CELEBRATIONES TRAGICOMICAE

TRAGI-COMIC
CELEBRATIONS

HORROR

If there is a realm that is inseparable from metal, it is unquestionably the world of horror, which covers all the themes connected to fear, suffering and death. From the gothic novel to pulp, from comics to exploitation films, the ideas and surreal, horrific imagery of these stories have always been a natural source for a style of music that aims to appear dark and violent, alternately morbid and fascinating. **Black Sabbath**, who are often referred to as the first metal group, drew their name from the 1963 horror film starring Boris Karloff. From the very birth of the genre, then, the link was made with horror films, and this connection would not diminish. The cover of *Sabbath Bloody Sabbath* is a concentration of all the most classic horrific and demonic motifs, from *The Exorcist* to *Rosemary's Baby*. On the cover of the album *Diary of a Madman*, **Ozzy Osbourne**, the group's vocalist, adopts the posture and look of a madman whose songs are his intimate diary. The conventions of the horror film occur in the aesthetic of thousands of groups, so intimately interconnected are they. Looking at the artwork of *Death Revenge* by the group **Exhumed**, one has the immediate impression that we are about to watch a movie, for the visual is designed like a poster, with a slasher arising from a cemetery in the depth of night at its centre. Ditto for the **Aborted** album *Bathos*, the cover of which shows some Lovecraftian 'cultists' above a house that is reminiscent of that featured in *The Amityville Horror*. Though often the codes may well be a little kitsch, as on *Holocausto de la Morte* (Holocaust of the Dead) by **Necrophagia**, they are nevertheless always effective and make us want to listen to the music that accompanies such visuals. In metal, monsters are literally family members. This is shown perfectly on the cover of *Zombie Attack* by **Tankard**, with its laughing monsters watching a horror film together. Sometimes there are even connections between horror films and music: besides the use of film samples as an introduction or as interludes, it is common for film soundtracks to have been composed by metal or prog rock groups. The soundtrack to *Giallo* directed by Dario Argento was made by the group **Goblin**, and that of *Queen of the Damned* brought together several metal groups. **Dani Filth**, the frontman of **Cradle of Filth**, even acted in a gore film entitled *Cradle of Fear*. And what about the leader of **White Zombie**, who became an iconic director of horror films under the name of Rob Zombie? These genres feed upon each other, and aim to treat the viewer/listener to a vivid, unforgettable journey, in the pure tradition of the ghost train, the Grand Guignol or a freak show.

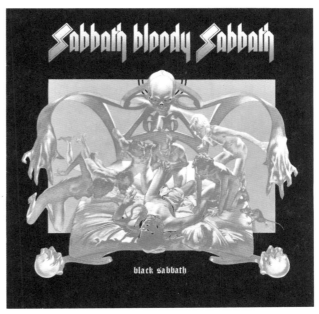

Tankard – *Zombie Attack*

Black Sabbath – *Sabbath Bloody Sabbath*

Aborted – *Bathos*

Exhumed – *Death Revenge*

ANDROGYNY

Among the many forces that make up the complex world of metal, one is certainly quite masculine: massive, heavy, aggressive and sometimes martial music that aims to dominate. Another force, though, is more ambiguous: sensual and deviant, bewitching and fascinating. These two forces may be in opposition, attract each other, or blend together, depending on the group involved. It is chiefly in the genres of glam rock and heavy metal that musicians began cross-dressing. While **David Bowie** played with this ambiguity to elevate it to the level of art and performance, in glam metal it was more a search for a rather fake outrageousness, which in the end barely lasted beyond the 2000s. The look of the frontman of **Twisted Sisters**, and the more androgynous one of **Poison**, disguise music whose themes and energy are purely masculine. They use a visual trick inherited from shock rock and its attitudes to immerse themselves in an aesthetic characteristic of the 1980s and, in the end, highly kitsch. These groups paved the way, almost despite themselves, for deeper reflection on questions of appearance, sexuality, and what was supposedly normal. In the post-heavy metal era, it was not until **Marilyn Manson** came on the scene that androgyny attained a much darker, more political aesthetic. **Manson** is a sort of evil twin of **Bowie**, using his appearance to take on the persona of almost fantastic creatures, capable of conveying his vitriolic messages against an extremely conservative America. The cover of his album *Mechanical Animals* shows him made up in a disturbing fashion, sporting breasts and a crotch that is on the borderline between the sexes. Here too, while an approach may divide opinion or be met with incomprehension, once a door has been opened, it stays open. From this perspective, it is fascinating to observe the Japanese visual kei scene, a heterogeneous musical genre that took androgynous aesthetics into spheres with few competitors in the West. Pioneers such as **X Japan** clearly showed their hand on the single *Orgasm*, blending outrageous make-up close to that of kabuki, paired with crazy peroxide hair and an overabundance of studded leather in an approach worthy

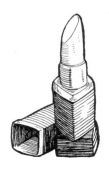

of black metal. From **Dir En Grey** to **Versailles**, whose guitarist **Hizaki** dresses and wears make-up like a young courtesan at the court of the Sun King, the range of possibilities seems endless. In Japanese culture, which has featured costume and make-up for centuries, cross-dressing seems to be a less political issue than it is in Western society, which is historically more conservative regarding such matters. While certain visual kei artists seek simply to play the role of imaginary characters to portray rich fantasy worlds, they nonetheless call into question stereotypes of appearance and sexuality.

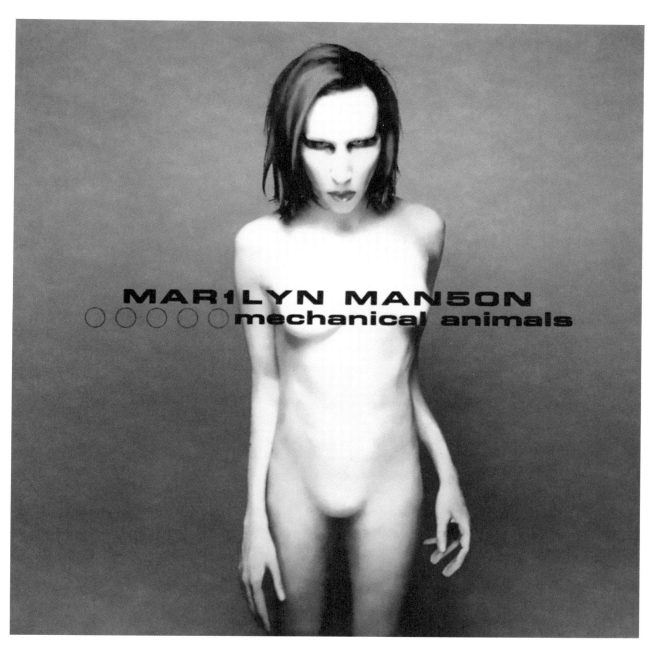

Marilyn Manson – *Mechanical Animals*
Poison – *Look What the Cat Dragged In*
Twisted Sister – *Under the Blade*

Although the album cover is often the main way in which a group can share their visual world, there are also promotional photographs, stage acts and music videos. These three formats make it possible to associate faces, attitudes and an aesthetic with a group's music. Some artists have seized upon these elements to make them embody other things, deciding to use these expressive spaces as a sort of theatrical stage. The use of masks in metal is especially frequent, in direct competition with electronic music. It is evident that a masked artist provokes a certain fascination. **Daft Punk** set a precedent by making full use of the enigma constituted by musicians who hid their identities. Who were they in their private lives? What message were their masks trying to convey? That which is hidden from our gaze fascinates us. Doubtless our attraction for this spectacular anonymity comes from the culture of the superhero, who hides their true identity to serve a cause that is beyond mere mortals. Of course, it is, above all, a matter of entertainment, and this practice comes directly from shock rock, as first introduced by **Alice Cooper**, **Kiss** and other stalwarts of that scene.

They put music and the appearance of those making it on the same plane. In the case of **Kiss**, we see clearly that make-up is a mask like any other. Some groups of the new generation have taken this practice further, adopting an aesthetic closer to the slasher or the 'cultist' than to a masked righter of wrongs. **Mushroomhead** fascinate with their masks, which change completely from one album to another. Other groups, such as **Ghost** and their frontman **Papa Emeritus**, follow shock rock tradition by dressing their heavy rock/metal in ecclesiastical decorum to perform a great hypnotic Mass (as well as allowing for discreet changes of line-up). **Gwar** play the schoolboy card with their grotesque, monstrous cosplays, but without ever

taking themselves seriously. But it was **Slipknot** that gave the mask prestige. With its ultra-violent, unstable music and the scary masks conceived as the musicians' evil alter egos, the arrival of their second album turned the standards of classic shock rock upside down. By taking on a new persona – the masks used by actors in antiquity – we can transcend our timidity and embody something that is beyond us, or even something that frightens us. The mask gives a certain strength and knows how to take advantage of the fascination it creates. An ideal and powerful passport to fear, dreams or the grotesque, the mask is not about to drop...

Slipknot – *Slipknot*
Alice Cooper – *Welcome to My Nightmare*
Kiss – *Kiss*

LEATHER

Leather is nothing more than the tanned skin of a dead animal that used to be hunted in days gone by. While it is sometimes brandished as a morbid trophy, the imaginary world associated with this material contains the idea that we absorb the power of the animal by wearing its skin. While leather features in certain groups with a medieval or fantasy aesthetic, it is modern black leather that has exploded in the nebula of metal. On *Ace of Spades*, **Motörhead** summon up the *pistolero* (gunslinger) from the movies of Sergio Leone: the group's members pose in the desert, covered in leather, wearing hats and ponchos under the sun. Their faces suggest a character as tough as the material they are wearing. The group gives the impression of being a gang of criminals about to attack a wagon train. It is but a step from the cowboy who has fallen on hard times to the hoodlum. To wear leather means to espouse tough music and a way of life on the margins of society. **Destructor** assert this explicitly with their album whose title is almost a slogan, *Forever in Leather*, and drive the point home with a simple visual of a leather jacket in close-up. While it says freedom and independence, leather can also suggest a threat. Many metal artists of this period have found themselves in the imaginary world of the 1960s hoodlum, a forerunner of decadent punk and the thief armed with a flick-knife. The cover of *Watch Out!* by **Living Death** illustrates this perfectly. It shows a band of bad boys ready to attack, fists up and covered with studded leather to inflict more pain when fighting. The gang appear in the smoke billowing from a manhole, as if their music was a punch you receive by surprise after losing your way and wandering into a dangerous alley. From James Dean to Marlon Brando playing a biker, leather has become associated with sexual energy – as though a wild desire went hand in hand with the thrill of a life on the wrong side of the law. It is also the stuff of domination and shady, underground sexual practices. Leather is the flagship material of the world of bondage and sadomasochism. It is as

if leather smelled of sulphur, as if this material aroused an urge in part of our reptilian brain. On the cover of *Unleashed in the East*, a live album recorded in Japan, **Rob Halford** of **Judas Priest** adapts this dark imaginary world of leather to extract its sexual side, posing with his arm raised, shirtless, in his leather jacket, sporting a policeman's helmet, as if to make the word *cuir* (leather) rhyme with 'queer'. Finally, along with the movies *Cruising* by William Friedkin and *Giallo* by Dario Argento, **Gama Bomb** play on the final aspect of leather: the idea of the killer. In a poster style that brings to mind the figure of a slasher, the group show a leather glove that is stopping a young woman from screaming, her eyes staring, wide with surprise. The title – *Give Me Leather* – emphasizes the point.

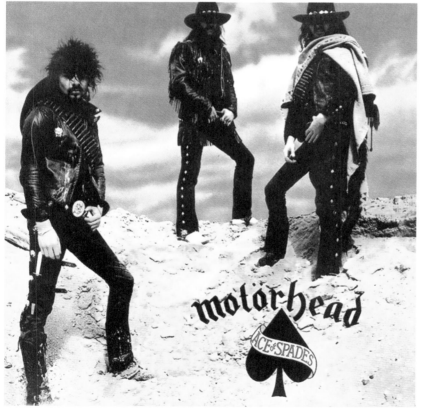

Destructor – *Forever in Leather*
Motörhead – *Ace of Spades*
Gama Bomb – *Give Me Leather*

CONCLAVE CURIOSITATUM

A CABINET OF
CURIOSITIES

Although the themes relating to lettering and groups' logos would deserve a codex of their own, they are often relegated to second place because the visual usually predominates. Yet certain groups have worked on their logo so as to make it dominant, even central. The band's logo is the only thing that remains common to all the albums. When a group is formed, a lot is at stake with its name: it will embody the line-up's entire identity. Since metal is a style of music that aims to inspire fascination tinged with fear, a logo must possess a certain stature. During the 1980s and 1990s, the logo in chromed metal had its moment of fame – from **Warning** with *Warning II* to **Metallica** with *Ride the Lightning* – in a style that was somewhere between science fiction and slasher film. Metal, and more broadly rock, are among the few styles of music where the logo has a real importance, and the culture of patches and tattoos is doubtless connected to this need groups have to devise their logos as emblems, badges that people might want to wear. The right logo can, to some extent, render your group iconic – immediately visually recognizable. Groups often even create their own characteristic typeface, to the point that you can find **Iron Maiden**'s typeface in some word-processing software. A logo is a very powerful space for personalization and can, depending on its form, deliver a message. Depending on whether your logo features pikes, esoteric symbols, dripping blood, or reflections in ice, you will send out a different message as to your approach and the world your music inhabits. The perfectly iconic logo of **Mayhem**, with its letter endings featuring bats' wings and the blasphemous inverted crosses hidden in its design, is enough in itself to intrigue us. Like the title of a horror film, the metal logo can get away with almost anything, even if it means pushing back the boundaries of what is reasonable in terms of publicity. Since a logo is nothing other than visual communication, it is supposed to be readable, clear, impactful – and memorable. Yet many groups have taken the design route in the 'wrong' direction, which is particularly original and fascinating. Therein lies the whole importance of logos, especially in black metal. Through the codes it has ended up establishing, black metal encourages the creation of logos that are as disturbing as possible, even if that means they are absolutely impossible to decipher unless you already know the band. Here, the logo is seen as a key giving entry to a world reserved only for those who have been initiated. The incomprehensible aspect of these designs shows an uncompromising, intransigent approach. As well as having a relatively unpronounceable name, the South African group **XAVLEGBM-AOFFFASSSSITIMIWOAMN-DUTROABCWAPWAEIIPPO-HFFFX** sport a logo that is completely illegible. In that very logo there is a desire to blow convention apart, which gives a foretaste of the music that awaits us. In grind metal, logos often become a sort of mess that is deliberately illegible – enough to drive any graphic designer crazy – and accompanied by putrid imagery. Here, the logo is an intentional act of visual aggression: the viewer is showered with nihilistic bad taste, which exudes a certain power through the rejection that the combined visual and logo provoke, even to the point of voluntarily denying themselves the slightest chance of being marketable. Quite often, the music lives up to this promise, what with its guttural howls and sordid ultra-violence.

Morbid Angel – *Gateways to Annihilation*
Mayhem – *Wolf's Lair Abyss*

GRAPHIC DESIGN

Although most of the albums cited in this codex have passed through the hands of a graphic designer to address the layout, lettering and printing, it is rare for an album sleeve's visuals to have been entirely created by one. Graphic design and visual communication are more akin to decorative and technical art than to the fine arts. Capitalism and marketing have taken over in order to make product packaging attractive to us, so much so that we tend to forget the artistic side of these disciplines. Graphic artists the world over are often frustrated that they have to depend on commercial imperatives in order to create their images. Album covers are thus one of the few places where graphic artists can express themselves freely, and even to play around with the traditional conventions of media, as on the albums *Vilosophe* and *Be All End All* by the group **Manes**. In some cases, we are not very far from a company logo, as with the second album by **Periphery**, entitled *This Time It's Personal*, or the album *Construct* by **Dark Tranquillity**. Modern typefaces are used, though their shapes are reworked and modified. Lettering is positioned in a balanced, original way – for, in everything from propaganda posters to brand logos, the impact of a legible and attractive graphic message is well known. On these album covers, we

have the feeling that the layout has been calculated down to the last pixel. The temptation to produce something that is too clean and precise, too justified, can sometimes render a visual too distant and lacking in humanity. This is a graphic style that is used by **Ulver** on *Blood Inside* and *1993–2003: 1st Decade in the Machines*. The use of graphic and layout software, highly technical and mathematical in character, dictates the aesthetic of these album covers, which from time to time exude a certain coldness due to their computerized precision. *One One One* by **Shining**, with its angular typeface and uniform fluorescent orange background, even has a certain austerity about it. For all that, there is in these albums something resolutely modern, which seeks to break free from classic metal. Here, what is intriguing is the diametrically opposite approach. The cover of *How the World Came to an End* by **Manes**, which combines militarist lettering with raster graphics, displays a dry, arid aesthetic that suits the album's title to perfection. However, it is probably **Liturgy** who win the prize with the artwork on *H.A.Q.Q.*, which looks like a cold, unsightly PowerPoint slide at a tedious seminar.

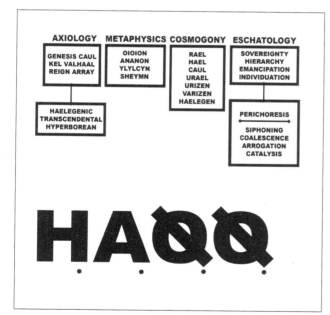

Ulver – *Blood Inside*
Shining – *One One One*
Liturgy – *H.A.Q.Q.*
For Today – *Wake*

Even though metal is one of the richest and most graphically codified genres, some groups opt for a radically different approach and present us with an abstract album cover. This approach – which does not show recognizable figures or objects – functions as a manifesto and is a sign of a group that aims to free themselves from tradition and claim they are in some sense avant-garde. It is commercially risky, for it makes no concessions to marketing. It is even common for such groups to withhold their name and that of the album from the cover, retaining only the image and its mysteries. There is a certain intransigence, a form of elitism, in daring to feature such a visual. The group are aiming only at those who will show curiosity and artistic openness. The potential listener has no iconic or at least familiar visual to get a purchase on. Seeing the sleeve – and title – of the album *ˣdʰĝʰm̥tós*, we understand that the group **Arkhaaik** want to leave us completely in the dark about the imaginary world into which they intend to invite us. We contemplate only texture and shapes… We pick up more a feeling, an ambiance, than a nod to a recognizable world. Other covers come close to the art brut (outsider art) of Jean Dubuffet, like the intriguing sleeve of *Universal Death Church* by **Lord Mantis**. It has an illegible, saturated, vibrant quality that takes us far from artistic conventionalism. The same goes for *Permanent Destitution* by **Hissing**: the mixture of techniques and textures, the superimposition of areas of colour reminiscent of screen printing – we cannot say what we are looking at, yet something has been communicated, a mental sensation that only abstract art allows us to experience, if we can agree to advance blindly and approach a work without being given the slightest direction. Abstract art allows our eyes to experience pareidolia, as in the artwork of the album *Blight Upon Martyred Sentience* by **Impetuous Ritual**, where we can imagine that we see a little owl, a Great Old One or some rock paintings. In a style that borders on the figurative, **Dreadnought**, with the album *Emergence Review*, use the device of a painting that at once reminds us of many things and of nothing in particular. Is it a body, a flower or a parasite? Only abstract art manages to leave us in this interpretative no-man's-land. This cryptic and sensory approach to the visual can allow us to give a shape to something indescribable. For example, the evanescent cover of *Weightless* by the group **Animals as Leaders** perfectly illustrates the album's title. The blurred, misty, ethereal visual they have chosen gives us a sensation of lightness and suspended time. Sometimes, figurative images are no longer enough to convey the emotions.

Lord Mantis – *Universal Death Church*
Arkhaaik – *$*d^h\hat{g}^h m tós$*

ARTISTIC PHOTOGRAPHY

Used extremely widely in advertising, photography sometimes leads us to forget its purely artistic character and the strange melancholy that can emanate from these frozen moments. Photography is the first tool for capturing reality. It is a technique in which the photographer's eye tends to turn an artistic gaze on to reality. Among the great classic subjects of photography, we find landscapes, nature – fauna and flora – portraits and the body. On the cover of the album *Is.Land*, **Time to Burn** show an out-of-focus bird in the foreground, and behind it a valley that stretches away as far as the eye can see, the whole in a magnificent, grainy black and white. On *The Mantle* by **Agalloch**, there is a statue of a stag shot from a low angle, its antlers blending with the branches of a tree in the background. In these images there is a faint melancholy, which suggests serious, vast, uncompromising music that seeks to invoke a form of reality and naturalism. **Deftones** take the opposite approach on *Gore*, whose title clashes with the unreal, almost soothing visual of dozens of pink flamingos captured by the camera as they take flight. While scenes of nature and animals induce a certain state of mind, it is often very different when the human body is depicted. The impact of a body in a photograph can make a statement about numerous political and social themes. On the cover of *Filler* by **Minor Threat**, the image of a tired, shabbily dressed body, slumped with head on knees as if recovering from a drinking binge, goes well with the album's music, which oscillates between punk and straight-edge hardcore, with a strong protest and anti-establishment character. Photography here serves to deliver a message: our music does not cheat; it is just like us, so much so that just a photo is enough to represent us. This is a very common custom in hardcore, whose entire mentality is based on a kind of authenticity and honesty. It is

a style of music that has the effect of a straight punch to the face. The concert photo is almost a cliché of the genre. As on the album *Start Today* by **Gorilla Biscuits**, a hardcore album cover often shows the group in mid-performance, in black and white. The shot must capture the intensity of the moment and all the energy it unleashes. Finally, a photo of the human body can be disturbing, in that it can show the fragility or decline of the flesh. The cover of *French Cancan* by the group **Carnival in Coal** is visually striking with its distended, almost scrawny bodies, which bring to mind famine and sickness, while blending the whole with a kind of icy, sinister eroticism. Photography possesses this truth, the quality of proof – what we see really existed – that painting has long coveted.

AGALLOCH
THE MANTLE

Gorilla Biscuits – *Start Today*
Minor Threat – *Filler*
Agalloch – *The Mantle*
Time to Burn – *Is.Land*
Carnival in Coal – *French Cancan*

SURREALISM

Of all the movements in art, surrealism is probably the one that has most left its mark on pop culture. It has become the vehicle for the strange, the grotesque and the improbable, and has greatly broadened the horizon of what is possible. Founded by the writer André Breton, surrealism was a movement in literature and painting without which there would have been no Giger or Beksiński. Its approach aimed to give creative control to psychological forces such as the subconscious and its offshoots – dreams, automatism and more. Although we tend to remember above all Dalí and Magritte for their strange and fascinating worlds, surrealism is a movement that liberated part of the creative process and allowed artists to draw on their nightmares, their fantasies and the depths of the self. Surrealism made it possible to present something that was figurative and impossible at the same time. It is a genre closely connected to fantasy and science fiction when it comes to the worlds it portrays. The album sleeve is one of the few formats that allow this surreal art to fully express itself, for it can take the liberty of being both poetic and disturbing, iconic and dreamlike. Sometimes the smallest thing is enough for an album cover to fit into this category, like the child in the artwork of *A Change of Seasons* by **Dream Theater**, who seems to be playing in the sand – except that the sand is, in fact, snow. The same goes for the eponymous album by **Tchornobog**, where we can discern an arid, mountainous moor with mountains towering over it. In its centre, a human eye surveys the moor with a mad gaze, like that of Sauron over Mordor. The desired effect – to show something beyond reality – is often achieved thanks to a distortion of the scale of things and structures: the size of the giant heads in white stone on *The Madness of Many* by **Animals as Leaders** is impossible, as are the floating pyramids filled with blue sky on *Fourth Dimension* by **Stratovarius**. Surrealism is a complex style of art that can quite quickly lapse into kitsch or poor taste. Everything depends on whether the artists succeed in invoking

that 'worrying strangeness' dear to Dalí, both visually and in their music. This is what **SUP** manage to do on *Hegemony*, where jellyfish shaped like wreaths of smoke escape from an erupting volcano. **Veil of Maya** also achieve this with their visually complex collage on *False Idol.* In order to have an effect, surrealist images often need to be close to *trompe-l'œil.* It is enough for a single element to be strange for the whole to become... surrealist! On *De-Loused in the Comatorium*, **Mars Volta** feature a doctored photograph worthy of Magritte, depicting a gold head on a plate, its mouth emitting light. In this type of work, there is always a visual dissonance that catches us unawares, just as dreams do so effectively.

SUP – *Hegemony*
Soilwork – *Natural Born Chaos*

The world of metal artworks is so unique in its themes and aesthetics that it almost deserves a place of its own in the history of art (in a world where art was not so hierarchical). There is no official name for the movement often referred to as the 'Dark Art Movement', which is descended directly from artists such as Hieronymus Bosch and Francisco de Goya, who were pioneers in the exploration of artistic darkness. More contemporary artists, such as Giger and Beksiński, have been plundered to illustrate metal albums, so perfectly does their style fit with the worlds that are conjured up. This deliciously sinister and limitless branch of art has made it possible to highlight as yet unseen visual worlds and, naturally, some artists have ended up specializing in the design of these album covers. It was probably with **Iron Maiden**, and their collaboration with the artist Derek Riggs (who created the covers featuring Eddie the Head), that people began to talk about cover artists as much as they talked about the band. Like Iron Maiden with Riggs, **Cannibal Corpse** worked almost exclusively with Vince Locke, as his unique gore style fitted perfectly with the group's world. As well as giving a certain coherence to a group's aesthetic, this approach has also created a sort of star system of cover designers. People dream of having a visual created by so-and-so: how many groups have fought over the talents of Necrolord and his covers featuring colours as blue as the dawn of time? How many have called on the immense talent of Dan Seagrave, whose complex art is unique and fantastic? His Lovecraftian architectural style is immediately recognizable, and confers on an album a mystical dimension that allows the music to take on an unparalleled aura, opening the doors to the world of the imagination with a single image. In a vein more akin to comics, it is impossible not to mention
Ed Repka, creator of dozens of thrash metal covers, whose handiwork is immediately recognizable. Thus, groups have ended up calling on iconic artists who, by their very involvement, succeed in giving the project a certain legitimacy. There are many who have attained this pantheon of specialists: John Baizley and his art deco style, Paolo Girardi and his apocalyptic organic paintings, Chris Moyen and his black-and-white Satanist drawings, Jeff Grimal and his almost-abstract paintings that play on light and materials, and, indeed, Førtifem, with their approach that is reminiscent of engraving… Although they are not all equally famous, it is definitively to all these artists that this book pays homage. Art knows no borders but it sometimes restricts itself in order to reach the widest possible audience. All these artists are among those who have pushed back its limits, for our darkest delight…

Baroness – *Purple*

Parlor – *Softly*

Dissection – *Storm of the Light's Bane*

Acknowledgements

We would like to thank Marie for her confidence and Alexandra for her time, as well as our respective communities, who for some years now have given us their support. This book exists thanks to all of you.

Album cover credits

p. 9 : *The Psychedelic Sounds of the 13th Floor Elevators* | 13th Floor Elevators | International Artists | © John Cleveland | 1966 • *Disraeli Gears* | Cream | Reaction | © Martin Sharp | 1967 • *Middle of Nowhere* | Acid King | Svart Records | © Tim Lehi | 2015 • *Axis : Bold as Love* | Jimi Hendrix Experience | Track Records | © Roger Law | 1967 ; p. 11 : *In the Darkness*| Paul Chain Violet Theater | Minotauro | © Edinform | 1986 • *We Live* | Electric Wizard | Rise Above Records | © Anthony J. Roberts | 2004 • *Master of Reality* | Black Sabbath | Vertigo | © Bloomsbury Group | 1971 ; p. 13 : *Black Widow* | Black Widow | CBS | © Rose Trengrove | 1970 • *Witchtanic Hellucinations* | Acid Witch | Razorback Records | 2008 • *Sacrifice* | Black Widow | CBS | © Circa & Rick Breach | 1970 • *Black Sabbath* | Black Sabbath | Vertigo | © Keef | 1970 • *She Was a Witch* | 1782 | Electric Valley Records | © Sscvlt | 2019 • *The Great Depression* | Witch Charmer | HeviSike Records | 2014 : p. 15 : *Inri* | Sarcófago | Cogumelo Produções | © Toninho Iron Bag | 1987 • *Witchcraft Destroys Minds and Reaps Souls* | Coven | Mercury | 1969 ; p. 17 : *Reinkaos* | Dissection | Black Horizon Music | 2006 • 666 | Aphrodite's Child | Vertigo | 1972 • *Sigil of Lucifer* | Imprecation | Negativity Records | © Daniel Shaw | 2010 ; p. 19 : *Infernal Chaos* | Quo Vadis | Metal Scrap Records | 2010 • Chaos Echoes | Bloody Sign | Blood Harvest | ©2009 Stefan Thanneur | 2010 • *Random Chaos* | Crimson Midwinter | Morbid Noizz Productions | © Michael Semprevivo | 1998 ; p. 21 : *Goat* | Nunslaughter | Revenge Productions | 2017 • *Give 'Em Hell* | Witchfynde | Rondelet Music & Records | 1980 • *Trampled Under Hoof* | Goatsnake | Southern Lord | 2004 ; p. 23 : *One Tail, One Head* | One Tail, One Head | Terratur Possessions | 2011 • *The Great Southern Trendkill* | Pantera | EastWest Records America | 1996 • *Love Hunter* | Whitesnake | United Artists Records | 1979 ; p. 25: *Entranced by Sound & Smoke* | Goat Bong | 2019 • *Lucifer's Fall* | Lucifer's Fall | Rotedoom Records | 2014 • *Regarde les hommes tomber* | Regarde les hommes tomber | Les Acteurs de l'Ombre Productions | © Førtifem | 2013 • *Six6Six* | Sacrilege | Pure Steel Records | 2015 ; p. 27 : *Of Fire and Stars* | Desert Near the End | Total Metal Records | © Remedy Art Design | 2019 • *Live Aus Berlin* | Rammstein | Motor Music | 1999 • *Branded and Exiled* | Running Wild | Noise | © Running Wild | 1985 ; p. 29 : *From Beer to Eternamix* | Ministry | 2014 • *Cracked Brain* | Destruction | • *Dopethrone* | Electric Wizard | Rise Above Records | © Tom Bagshaw | 2000 ; p. 31 : *The Morning After* | Tankard | Noise International | © Sebastian Krüger | 1988 • *Trúbadóirí Óta an Diabhail* | Urfaust | Ván | © Anthony J. Roberts | 2013 • *Beast of Bourbon* | Tankard | AFM Records | © Sebastian Krüger | 2004 ; p. 35 : *Upon This Rock* | Larry Norman | Capitol Records | © David Coleman | 1970 • *Walkin' in Faith* | Angelica | Intense Records | © Jeff Foster | 1990 • *Into a New Dimension* | Divinefire | Nexus | © Rivel Records | 2006 ; p. 39 : *In the Heart of the Rainforest* | Striborg | Finsternis Productions | © Sin-nanna | 2001 • *Suicide Forest* (demo 2016) | After Death Alone | 2016 • *Forgotten Legends* | Drudkh | Supernal Music | © Season of Mist | 2003 • *Wyrd* | Elvenking | AFM Records | 2004 ; p. 41 : *Eternal Winter's Prophecy* | Catamenia | Massacre Records | 2000 • *An Overdose of Death* | Toxic Holocaust | Relapse Records | © Halseycaust | 2008 • *Sons of the Jackal* | Legion of the Damned | Massacre Records | 2007 ; p. 43 : *Frost* | Enslaved | Osmose Productions | © Svein Grønvold | 1994 • *Twilight of the Gods* | Bathory | Black Mark Production | © Quorthon | 1991 • *The Force of the Ancient Land* | Eldamar | Northern Silence Productions | 2016 • *Likferd* | Windir | Head Not Found | 2003 ; p. 45 : *At the Heart of Winter* | Immortal | Osmose Productions | © JP Fournier | 1999 • *1184* | Windir | Head Not Found | 2001 ; p. 47 : *Lunar Deflagration* | Nuit Noire | Creations of the Night | 2004 • *In the Nightside Eclipse* | Emperor | Candlelight Records | © Necrolord | 1994 ; p. 49 : *Triumph of Death* | Hellhammer | Prowling Death Records | 1983 • *Conspiracy* | King Diamond | Roadrunner Records | © Studio Dzyan | 1989 • *Pure Holocaust* | Immortal | Osmose Productions | 1993 ; p. 53 : *Some Enchanted Evening* | Blue Öyster Cult | Columbia | 1978 • *See You in Hell* | Grim Reaper | Ebony Records | © Garry Sharpe-Young | 1983 • *Follow the Reaper* | Children of Bodom | Spinefarm Records | © Sami Saramäki | 2000 ; p. 55 : *The Graveless Remains* | Disma | Profound Lore Records | © Daniel Shaw | 2017 • *Fire in the Brain* | Oz | Wave | 1983 ; p. 57 : *Hordes of Zombies* | Terrorizer | Season Of Mist | © Doomsday Graphics | 2012 • *Hell on Earth* | Toxic Holocaust | Nuclear War Now! Productions | © Ed Repka | 2005 • *Reign of Rotten Flesh* | Zombie Riot | Unholy Fire Records | 2018 ; p. 59 : *An Epiphany of Hate* | Master | FDA Rekotz | 2016 • *Beyond the Dark Border* | Horrid | Dunkelheit Produktionen | © Þorvaldur Guðni Sævarsson | 2017 ; p. 61 : *Severed Survival* | Autopsy | Peaceville | 1990 ; p. 63 : *Instruments of Torture* | Brodequin | Ablated Records | 2001 • *The Impious Doctrine* | Carnivorous Voracity | Amputated Vein Records | © Daemorph | 2015 ; p. 65 : *Hell's Domain* | Hell's Domain | Punishment 18 Records | © Edward J. Repka | 2013 • *Een pathologie van de geneesheer* | Psyche | Consistentis Veritatis Peremptoria | 2018 ; p. 67 : 'Mein Teil' | Rammstein | Universal | 2004 • *Ultimo Mondo Cannibale* | Impetigo | Wild Rags Records | © Jim Reising | 1990 ; p. 73 : *They Ride Along* | Hagzissa | Iron Bonehead Productions | © Bentrella | 2019 • *Carpathia: A Dramatic Poem* | The Vision Bleak | Prophecy Productions | © Łukasz Jaszak | 2005 ; p. 75 : *Angst* | Todtgelichter | Aural Music / Code666 | © Y | 2010 • *A Social Grace* | Psychotic Waltz | Sub-Sonic | © Mike Clift | 1990 ; p. 77 : *The Best of Helsinki Vampires* | The 69 Eyes | Nuclear Blast | © Jari Salo | 2013 • *A Catharsis For Human Illness* | Vlad Tepes | Drakkar Productions | © VarvLoar1476 Arz | 2018 • *Pride of Older Times* | Basarab | 2003 ; p. 79 : *The Empires of Death* | Puteraeon | Growls from the Underground | 2017 • *Consumed by Elder Sign* | Innsmouth | Abysmal Sounds | © Mark Appleton | 2014 • *Get Thothed Vol. 1* | Arkham Witch | Metal On Metal Records | © Jowita Kaminska | 2015 ; p. 81 : *EOD: A Tale of Dark Legacy* | The Great Old Ones | Season of Mist | © Jeff Grimal | 2017 • *Convocation of Crawling Chaos* | Cruciamentum | Nuclear Winter/Martyrdoom | © Bad News Brown | 2009 • *Gateway to the Antisphere* | Sulphur Aeon | Ván/Imperium Productions | © Ola Larsson | 2015 • *Swallowed by the Ocean's Tide* | Sulphur Aeon | Imperium Productions | © Ola Larsson | 2012 ; p. 83 : *Overkill* | Motörhead | Bronze | © Joe Petagno | 1979 • *Powerslave* | Iron Maiden | EMI | © Derek Riggs | 1984 • *Orgasmatron* | Motörhead | GWR Records | © Joe Petagno | 1986 ; p. 87 : *Relayer* | Yes | Atlantic | Cover Painting and Logos by and © Roger Dean 1974 and 2018 | 1974 • *Skys over Westeros* | Skroth | Dethbridge Records | 2014 ; p. 89 : *Tales from the Twilight World* | Blind Guardian | No Remorse Records / Virgin | © Andreas Marschall | 1990 • *Unveiling the Essence* | Cirith Gorgor | Osmose Productions | © Kris Verwimp | 2001 • *Music Inspired by Lord of the Rings* | Bo Hansson | Charisma | © Jane Furst | 1972 ; p. 91 : *Crystal Logic* | Manilla Road | Roadster Records | © Cinda Hughes & John Jinks | 1983 • *Noble Savage* | Virgin Steele | Cobra | 1985 • *Hard Attack* | Dust | Kama Sutra | © Frank Frazetta | 1972 ; p. 93 : *The Armor of Ire* | Eternal Champion | No Remorse Records | © Adam Burke | 2016 • *The Anthology of Steel* | Medieval Steel | Sur Records | © Danny Umfess | 1984 • *None but the Brave* | Ironsword | Shadow Kingdom Records | © Victor Costa | 2015 • *Wargods of Metal* | Sacred Steel | Metal Blade Records | © Michael Bähre | 1998 • *Krvestřeb* | Maniac Butcher | Pussy God Records | © Barbarüd | 1997 ; p. 95 : *Tales of Ancient Prophecies* | Twilight Force | 2013 • *Rising* | Dream Spirit | Infected Blood Records | 2016 • *Asia* | Asia | Geffen Records | © Roger Dean | 1982 ; p. 97 : *Reign in Supreme Darkness* | Vargrav | Werewolf Records | © Misanthropic | 2019 • *The Wizard* | Merlin | The Company | 2017 • *Limbonic Art* | In Abhorrence Dementia | Nocturnal Art Productions | © Morfeus | 1997 • *Demons and Wizards* | Uriah Heep | Bronze | Cover Painting and Logos by and © Roger Dean 1972 and 2018 | 1972 • *Red Queen to Gryphon Three* | Gryphon | Transatlantic Records | © Dan Pearce | 1974 ; p. 99 : *Rock'n'Troll* | Litvintroll | BMA Group | 2009 • *Drep De Kristne* | Troll | Damnation | © Alex Kurtagic | 1996 ; p. 101 : *Keeper of the Seven Keys: Part II* | Helloween | Noise International | © Edda & Uwe Karczewski | 1988 • *A Knight at the Opera* | Nanowar of Steel | 2014 ; p. 105 : *SETI* | The Kovenant | Nuclear Blast | © Joachim Luetke | 2003 • *God is an Automaton* | Sybreed | Listenable Records | © Seth Siro Anton | 2012 • *Slave Design* | Sybreed | Jerkov Musiques / Reality Entertainment | © Mark Eikasia & Sybreed | 2004 ; p. 107 : *Steel the Light* | Q5 | Albatross Records | 1984 • *Hall of the Mountain Grill* | Hawkwind | United Artists Records | © Barney Bubbles | 1974 ; p. 109 : *Darkspace I* | Darkspace | Haunter of the Dark | 2003 • *Pupil of the Searing Maelstrom* | Almyrkvi | Ván | © Joseph Deegan | 2016 ; p. 111 : *Drone Activity* | Ulver | House of Mythology | © Wolframgraphik & Paschalis Zervas | 2019 • *S/2004 S3* | 01101111011101100110111001101001 | Pathologically Explicit Recordings | 2017 • *Transfer* | SUP | Revelation / Pias France | © Laurent Bessault | 1996 • *Nothing* | Meshuggah | Nuclear Blast | 2002 ; p. 115 : *Romulus* | Ex Deo | Nuclear Blast | © Rob Kimura | 2009 • *Die You Heathen, Die!* | Robespierre | Buried By Time and Dust Records | 2011 • *Antichrist Rise to Power* | Departure Chandelier | Nuclear War Now! Productions | 2019 • *To the Nameless Dead* | Primordial | Metal Blade Records | © A.A. Nemtheanga / Paul McCarroll / Unhinged Art | 2007 • *Jehanne* | Abduction | Finisterian Dead End | © Paul-Antoine de La Boulaye | 2020 ; p. 117 : *Citadelle* | Citadelle | Impious Desecration Records | 2016 • *The Power and the Glory* | Gentle Giant | WWA Records | © Cream | 1974 • *He Who Was Lost in Battle* | Ritual Flail | AHPN Records | © Arturas Slapsys | 2019 • *Destiny Calls* | Chevalier | (p) 2019 CRUZ DEL SUR MUSIC SRL / GATES OF HELL RECORDS | © Patrick Zöller / Karmazid | 2019 ; p. 119 : *A Passage to the Towers* | Darkenhöld | Ancestrale Production | © Claudine Vrac | 2010 • *Castellum* | Darkenhöld | Those Opposed Records / Les Acteurs de l'Ombre Productions | © Claudine Vrac | 2014 • *Far Away from the Sun* | Sacramentum | Adipocere Records | © Necrolord | 1996 ; p. 121 : *The Crusher* | Amon Amarth | Metal Blade Records | © Thomas Ewerhard & Tom Thiel | 2001 • *Blood Fire Death* | Bathory | Under One Flag | 1988 • *Iron* | Ensiferum | Spinefarm Records | 2004 • *Hammerheart* | Bathory | Noise International | © Sir Frank Dicksee | 1990 ; p. 123 : *Yggdrasil* | Krilloan | 2020 • *Yggdrasil Burns* | Kurgan | Massacre Records | 2019 • *Yggdrasil : Journey throughout the Nine Worlds* | Darkened Winter | Infernal Kommando Records | 2013 ; p. 125 : *Incantations Through the Gates of Irkalla* | Akhenaten | Murdher Records / Satanath Records / Darzamadicus Records | 2015 • *Sphynx* | Melechesh | Osmose Productions | 2003 • *Emissaries* | Melechesh | Osmose Productions | © John Coulthart / Herbaut / Eblis / Szpajdel / Paul Guess / 2006 • *Those Whom the Gods Detest* | Nile | courtesy of Nuclear Blast & Nile c/o World Entertainment Inc. | © Michał 'Xaay' Loranc | 2009 • *Undama Tath'hur Al Shams Min Al Gharb* | Narjahanam | HAARBN Productions | 2007 • *Age of Ascendancy* | Tamerlan Empire | Metal Hell Records | © APRA AMCOS | 2018 ; p. 127 : *Ghastly Funeral Theatre* | Sigh | Cacophonous Records | 1997 • *Scorn Defeat* | Sigh | Deathlike Silence Productions | 1993 ; p. 129 : *La Caida de Tonatiuh* | Impureza | Season Of Mist | © Johann Bodin | 2017 • *Quarterpast* | MaYaN | Nuclear Blast | © Stefan Heilemann | 2011 ; p. 131 : *Hoist the Black Flag* | Iron SeaWolf | © Owen Evans | 2016 • *Under Jolly Roger* | Running Wild | Noise International | 1987 • *Pilgrimage* | Zed Yago | RCA | © Kai Bardeleben | 1989 ; p. 133 : *The Boats of the Glen Carrig* | Ahab | Napalm Records | 2015 • *Barton's Odyssey* | Atlantis Chronicles | Apathia Records | © Pär Olofsson | www.parolofsson.se |2016 • *The Call of the Wretched Sea* | Ahab | Napalm Records | 2006 • *The Divinity of Oceans* | Ahab | Napalm Records | © Peter Paul Rubens / Théodore Géricault | 2009 ; p. 135 : *Battle Breed* | Bodyfarm | Cyclone Empire | 2015 • *Street War Metal Kommand* | Split Abigail / Hate Kommand | Deathtrash Armageddon | 2008 • *Black Metal Ist Krieg* | Nargaroth | No Colours Records | 2001 • *Battle Metal* | Turisas | Century Media | © Niklas Sundin | 2004 ; p. 137 : *Marcellin s'en va-t'en guerre* | FT17 | 2016 • *Operation Wintersturm* | Endstille | Twilight | 2002 • *The Great War* | Sabaton | Nuclear Blast | © Peter Sallai | 2019 • *Until the War is Won* | ShadowKiller | Pure Steel Records | 2015 ; p. 139 : *Cherno* | Kursk | UHO Production | © Vesa Ranta | 2008 • *Agent Orange* | Sodom | Steamhammer | © Andreas Marschall | 1989 ; p. 141 : *The Return of the Filth Hounds* | Tank | Rising Sun Productions | 1998 • *Trumpet of Triumph* | Godless Rising | Moribund Records | © Chris Moyen | 2010 • *Panzer Division Marduk* | Marduk | Osmose Productions | © Dauthus | 1999 • *War Without End* | Warbringer | Century Media | 2008 ; p. 145 : *Street Trash* | Enhancer | Barclay | 2003 • *Promo'17* | The Worst Doubt | Straight & Alert Records | © Singemongol | 2017 • *Cold Street Homicide* | Machete 187 | One Life One Crew | 2016 ; p. 147 : *Beware of Metal* | IntoxXxicateD | Sade Records | 2009 • *Heavy Metal Chainsaw* | Metalucifer | Iron Pegasus Records | 2001 • *Violent Mosh* | Violator | Kill Again Records | 2004 • *Trash Metal Victory* | Traitor | Fistfuck Records | 2009 • *Spread the Fire* | Fueled by Fire | Annialation Records | 2006 ; p. 149 : *Speed Metal Sentence* | Cranium | Necropolis Records | © Ola Larsson | 1999 • *Blind Trust* | Sudden Rage | Coyote Records & Severed Records | 2014 ; p. 151 : *Burial of Self* | Aurora Disease | 2018 • *Lifelover* | Dekadens | Osmose Productions | 2009 ; p. 153 : *Attak* | KMFDM | Metropolis | © Brute! | 2002 • *City* | Strapping Young Lad | Century Media | 1996 • *Filth Pig* | Ministry | Warner Bros. Records | © Paul Elledge | 1995 ; p. 155 : *Family Man* | Black Flag | SST Records & Freeway Records | © Raymond Pettibon | 1984 • *You are One* | Unity | Wishingwell Records | © Gavin Oglesby | 1985 • *The Day the Country Died* | Subhumans | Spiderleg Records | © Nick Lant | 1982 • *Nailbomb* | Point Blank | Roadrunner Records | 1994 ; p. 157 : *Toxic Waste* | Municipal Waste x Toxic Holocaust | Tankcrimes | © Andrei Bouzikov | 2012 • *High on Radiation* | Reactory | Iron Shield Records | 2014 ; p. 159 : *Majestic Brewing Order* | Charm Charm Chu | Dying Legion | © Uncle 3 | 2014 • *Masquerade in Blood* | Sodom | Steamhammer | © Peter Dell & Andreas Marschall | 1995 • *Cabaret de la guillotine* | Angelus Apatrida | Century Media | © Gyula Havancsak | 2018 • *For Whose Advantage?* | Xentrix | Roadracer Records | © Brian Burrows | 1990 • *Two-Faced* | Tankard | Noise International | © Sebastian Krüger | 1993 • *Think This* | Toxik | Roadracer Records | © Ed Repka | 1989 ; p. 163 : *Zombie Attack* | Tankard | Noise International | © James Warhola | 1986 • *Sabbath Bloody Sabbath* | Black Sabbath | WWA Records | © Drew Struzan | 1973 • *Bathos* | Aborted | Century Media | © Coki Greenway | 2017 • *Death Revenge* | Exhumed | Relapse Records | © Orion Landau | 2017 ; p. 165 : *Mechanical Animals* | Marilyn Manson | Nothing Records | 1998 • *Look What the Cat Dragged In* | *Poison* | Enigma Records & Capitol Records | 1986 • *Under the Blade* | Twisted Sister | Secret Records | Avec l'aimable autorisation de Warner Music UK Ltd | © Fin Costello | 1982 ; p. 167 : *Slipknot* | Slipknot | Roadrunner Records | 1999 • *Welcome to My Nightmare* | Alice Cooper | Atlantic | © Pacific Eye & Ear | 1975 • *Kiss* | Kiss | Casablanca | © Joel Brodsky | 1974 ; p. 169 : *Forever in Leather* | Destructor | Auburn Records | 2007 • *Ace of Spades* | Motörhead | Bronze | © Allan Ballard | 1980 • *Give Me Leather* | Gama Bomb | AFM Records | © Rory McGuigan | 2018 ; p. 173 : *Gateways to Annihilation* | Morbid Angel | Earache | © Dan Seagrave | 2000 • *Wolf's Lair Abyss* | Mayhem | Misanthropy Records & Soulseller Records | © Kerri | 1997 ; p. 175 : *Blood Inside* | Ulver | Jester Records | © Trine + Kim Design Studio | 2005 • *One One One* | Shining | Indie Recordings | © Trine + Kim Design Studio | 2013 • *H.A.Q.Q.* | Liturgy | YLYLCYN | © Trine + Kim Design Studio | 2019 • *Wake* | For Today | Nuclear Blast | © Dave Quiggle | 2015 ; p. 177 : *Universal Death Church* | Lord Mantis | Profound Lore Records | 2019 • _*dʰgʷʰm̥tós_ | Arkhaaik | Iron Bonehead Productions | 2019 ; p. 179 : *Start Today* | Gorilla Biscuits | Revelation Records | 1989 • *Filler* | Minor Threat | Dischord Records | 1981 • *The Mantle* | Agalloch | The End Records | © John Haughm | 2002 • *Is.Land* | Time to Burn | Basement Apes Industries | © *Drew | 2007 • *French Cancan* | Carnival in Coal | Kodiak Records | © Boris Steam | 1999 ; p. 181 : *Hegemony* | SUP | Holy Records | © Matthieu Carton | 2008 • *Natural Born Chaos* | Soilwork | Nuclear Blast | © Travis Smith | 2002 ; p. 183 : *Purple* | Baroness | Abraxan Hymns | © Aaron Horkey | 2015 • *Storm of the Light Bane* | Dissection | Nuclear Blast & EastWest | © Necrolord | 1995 • *Softly* | Parlor | Hell Vice I Vicious Records | © Førtifem